Turn Left at the Big Oak

A Selection of Short Stories

By

Deborah Tilson Clark

To my mother,
Evelyn Louise Hyler Tilson,
who has kept me on the straight and narrow,
made me upright and honest,
and never let me get above my raising,
and
to my father,
Rudolph Lincoln Tilson,
who took me with him on the milk truck,
fell asleep while I played Beethoven,
and gave me away to a man whom he and I both trusted.

Thank you both, for everything, for ever.
Deb

Special thanks to Jessie and Catherine for their
generous sharing of artistic talents.

Published by Human Error Publishing
www.humanerrorpublishing.com
paul@humanerrorpublishing.com

Cover design
by
Catherine Schrenker

Illustrations
by
Jessie Tilson Clark

Table of Contents

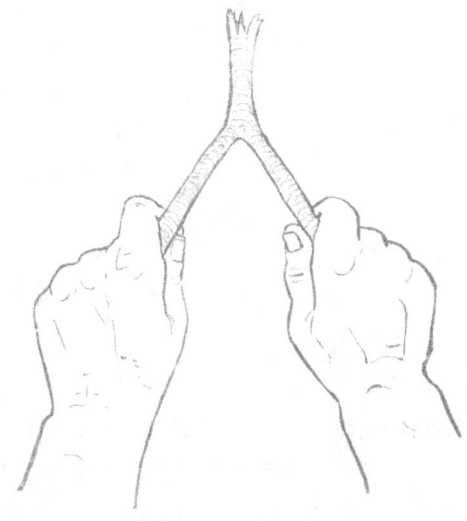

Dowsing

Sam Coldiron is known for being a dowser.

That's how he came to be in the woods that cold March afternoon with a forked cherry branch held in both hands, with me following while two county deputies and the sheriff waited by the road.

Water-witch, dowser, call them what you will, some people have the ability to find water. Actually, most men – and a few women – have the ability to use a tool, be it a tree branch or copper rods or just their outstretched hands, to sense and follow underground water. Some men can find not only underground water, but almost any kind of hidden object. In this day and age, "reason" rules and everything that's not explainable by scientific method is classified as ignorance, superstition, bad movie magic or, by the fundamentalist or old-fashioned, witchcraft, and most men don't know they have the ability. They haven't even heard of such a thing, so they've never tried, to see if they can do it.

Or they won't admit it.

But Sam Coldiron is the scion of a line of water-finders going back more than 150 years. He's known he has it – this gift, or talent, or curse – since he was four years old, and he knows how to use it. He never advertised and he never made a big deal out of it and most people don't know that he has more than a simple knack for finding a springhead or where the creek went, when it went underground.

He can find other things, too. One day someone in the Highlands County Sheriff's Department remembered the Coldiron reputation and asked Sam for help.

I was sitting at Sam's kitchen table when he got the call.

"Hello?" Sam's voice was low and grumbly, roughened by 45 years of smoking and even more by talking in a slow and thoughtful way and never letting emotion push his voice into a higher register or faster speed.

He paused, and I could hear a man's voice coming through the old-fashioned, corded receiver. Sam said the newer ones were so small he couldn't hold them to his ear with his shoulder, if he had to write down something a caller was telling him. So he kept the old phone on the wall in his kitchen, with the extra-long cord that would stretch all the way into the living room.

"Well." Sam put a period at the end of the word. "Yes. I believe I can do that, if I know the general area to look in, and if the body isn't too far decayed."

Body? I started paying attention, trying to hear what the little voice in the phone was saying.

"Deathbed confession..." I heard in the tiny, empty voice. "May be nothing, but... owe it..."

"Going to be rainy tomorrow," Sam said. That wasn't magic. That was paying attention to the Weather Channel, something I knew Sam liked to do. "How about Monday?"

Mumble, mumble, mumble from the phone.

"All right then. Nine o'clock, Taylor's Ridge. See you, Jimmy."

"Jimmy Jones?" I asked, naming the deputy who had graduated high school with Sam's second son, Phillip.

"Yep." Sam didn't waste a lot of words.

"Who's dead on Taylor's Ridge?" I asked. I'd learned years ago that if I pretended I knew more than I did or was supposed to, I could get more information from the close-mouthed Coldiron men than I'd get by asking outright. I'd also found that sometimes, I really did not want to know what they were trying to keep me from knowing.

"Maybe nobody." Sam scooted the pack of Camels out of his shirt pocket, shook one loose, put it in his mouth. He lit it with a small wooden match from the box he kept on the kitchen table. I knew he carried a disposable lighter in his pocket, but if he was at home, Sam used matches. He claimed he could smell the petroleum in the plastic lighters, and that it tainted his tobacco. As if.

I didn't say anything about the cigarette. Sam knew I wished he and Phillip both would quit. We'd argued about it quietly, for years.

"Some man died in County Memorial last week. Before he passed, he claimed he'd seen two men hiding a body up on Taylor's Ridge."

"When?"

"Last fall, early winter. Said the leaves were all on the ground."

It was early spring now. Whatever had happened - might have happened – happened five months ago. "Waited a while to inform the authorities, didn't he?"

"Some people want to unload before they leave," Sam said. He tapped his cigarette into the ashtray in the middle of the table. Other people have salt and pepper shakers or a sugar bowl or maybe even flowers; but Sam Coldiron has an ashtray. Old-fashioned, this one was, with a plaid fabric bottom like a beanbag and a metal top like a bowl. Sam kept it clean, dumping the butts and wiping it with crumpled newspaper several times a day.

Conversations with Sam move at a slower pace than most people can tolerate. He thinks things through before he commits to saying them out loud. Once said, Sam rarely tries

11

to take words back, or has to apologize for them. Eventually, he suggested, "Some people get mixed up, when they're getting ready to cross over. Might not be anything to this."

I waited for a while before answering. You get into the habit, living near these men. "Maybe he was protecting whoever was doing the hiding."

Sam tapped ash. "Or was afraid of them."

I thought about that, and decided that if the informant had been afraid, whoever uncovered the body – if there was one – perhaps should be, too. I didn't say this out loud. If arguing with Sam about cigarettes was fruitless, trying to deflect him from doing what he'd committed to doing was utterly pointless. Instead, I offered, "I didn't know you could find bodies."

"Can. Easier than things."

"What?"

"People used to ask us to find things: lost keys, wallets. A shotgun, once." He smiled a little at that memory. "Usually not a lot of luck with things. It's like there's not enough energy to them, or something."

Sam was being unusually garrulous. I like to think that he talks to me more than to most people. Everyone respects Sam and a great many people are fond of him, but few people are close to him. I want to be close, and feel warmed when he talks to me like this.

"Sam, what does it feel like, to dowse for things?"

He took his time. Of course. Finished the cigarette and quashed it thoroughly before answering.

"Water's easy. It's always there; it floats up about as much as it flows downhill. Cold, tingly. It's almost like you can feel the scent of it.

"Things – objects – well, it depends. Sometimes I've thought most man-made things can't really be felt, unless they've been handled so much, or been held in such... emotion, that it's packed the charge." Sam paused here, maybe to give me a chance to react, but there was nothing I wanted

12

to say. Most people either want to ignore what Sam can do or they want to be in on it, nosing around, asking a zillion questions and wanting Sam to show them how. They want to get a feel of the magic. A lot of people want there to be magic in the world. There's a lot of sad, lonely people around, these days. Me, I've lived with this family a long time, and I know they are as down-to-earth as spit. What they do is real, but it's like having a good eye for design or being able to instantly understand a map. It's easy to do but hard to explain. It's the way their minds are made. Maybe not many people are made like that, but more are than are likely to realize it or admit it. Too many hassles. And the last thing the Coldiron men want to do, usually, is dig around in their psyches, trying to figure out what makes them the way they are.

"If you're asking what I feel about doing it, well... Sometimes I feel real good. I like finding water for people. It's an honest and helpful thing, to find good water. So of course, fewer and fewer people ask me for that kind of help." He smiled again, in my direction, and I warmed. "But dowsing for most other stuff is... Sometimes it's... like I'm feeding their greed. Greed for the thing they're looking for, or greed for my work. Some people just want to see me do it."

Sam pushed the ashtray to the center of the table and leaned back in his chair. End of conversation. But I hated to let go of this time with Sam, so I asked another question. "What about finding bodies?"

Sam looked at me, and then away. He looked at his hand where it rested on the oilcloth-covered table. I'd bought that oilcloth at Dollar General and had spread it to cover where the Formica had started to be worn through. Sam didn't look up when he answered. "Depends," he said. "Sometimes, it's just a feeling of... rot. Everything rots, all the time, and it's all around. But with something as big as a human, the weight of it somehow tells what it is. Most of the time the bodies are so far down in the ground, it's barely there. And the... I don't know what to call it, energy, I guess...

13

is okay. Just natural. But sometimes the energy is bad. I don't know whether it's the way the person was in life, or the way he died. Maybe either. Or neither."

"This one is likely to be bad, isn't it?"

Sam didn't look up or answer, and the radio came on. Sam doesn't watch much television and cannot abide what he calls the "stringy" music they play on the NPR station out of Charlottesville, but he has a passion for the news produced by National Public Radio. He has a timer that plugs into the wall outlet and the radio plugs into that, and every day at exactly four o'clock, the radio clicks on and the eight notes of music that introduce "All Things Considered" leap into the room like the trumpet call of Gabriel.

I knew about the timer and the music, but it still made me jump and mutter "shit" under my breath. Sam smiled again, and more to cover up how I felt about that smile than because I was really peeved, I got up and said, "Well, time to go get supper." The radio woman's voice marched into the room, important and sure. I felt Sam's smile on my back as I went through his kitchen door. I put my jacket on to help keep it warm against me as I got into the car to drive to my house, where I would fix supper for my husband, Sam's son Phillip.

My way home from Sam's took me past the VDOT station where my father and my husband work, and I saw both their pickups in the parking lot. That told me they were finally working on the new bridge over Culbertson creek. Two months earlier, after a series of hard winter storms, one of the old, one-lane bridges in the county had been lifted by the swollen creek that – usually -- ran beneath it and set down in the adjoining pasture. Since then, the crew had worked to build up and stabilize the creekbanks, tried to move the old bridge back into place, broken the old bridge, and waited for permission and funding from the county and then the state, to replace the bridge. Every workday during that waiting period, Phillip had walked in our door at 5:12 exactly. I knew that the only thing that would keep Phillip from his usual routine was overtime on the job, and that if he was going to have to work late, there would be a message from him on our phone machine at home, letting me know.

I also drove past the sheriff's office, and, on a whim generated by the empty parking space right in front of the door as well as my conversation with Sam and the knowledge that I could delay making the usual hot supper for Phillip, I turned in, parked, and went in.

Jimmy was leaning against the edge of one desk, arms crossed on his chest and his ankles crossed in front of him, looking at Krystal, the dispatcher, who was laughing, seated behind another desk. They looked up as I walked in.

"Hi," I offered.

"Hey, Michelle, come in out of the weather," Jimmy said.

"Well, the weather's not so bad, maybe I should just stay out," I said, smiling. "Is Sheriff Dolinger in?" I asked, very casually.

Jimmy stood up and hooked a hand over the butt of the pistol loaded in his belt, making the leather creak in a manly way. "Is this social or business?" he asked. He made me think of a little boy, trying to stand up straight and look tall.

"Bout half of both," I said. Krystal and Jimmy waited, but I didn't offer more. Finally, just a couple of seconds later than she should have, Krystal said, "I'll see if he's available," and held down a button on the intercom. "Sheriff?" She used the diction that dispatchers must have to learn to be considered official. After hearing a gruff "Yeah?" from the box, she continued, "Michelle Coldiron is here to see you."

There was a four-second pause, then the voice said, "Send her in."

Krystal leaned back, looked up, and said by rote, "Down the hall, last door on the right."

"Thanks," I said, and strolled away. I felt their eyes on

my back as I walked down the hall.

The last door was open, and Sheriff Dolinger was standing up when I looked in. The Dolingers have been drop-in friends of our family for as long as I can remember, and members of our church, but for some reason, that day, I tried to look at him without the filter of our long relationship. Backlit by the light from the window behind him, I saw a tall man with a straight back and a not-too-big pot belly. He stood up straight, moved deliberately, seemed solid on the ground. He's been sheriff of Highlands for nearly 20 years, and although the brown and tan uniform fits him well, it was easy to see he would be more comfortable in jeans and flannel shirts. He is of Sam's generation, which is also my father's generation, and maybe that's one reason I tend to trust these guys, with their inward-looking gazes and live-and-let-live philosophies. Sheriff Dolinger told me once, years ago, that he wished he didn't have to wear his pistol as part of his uniform. "If I don't have it, people I'm talking to are more relaxed; trouble just isn't as likely to develop," he said. "Just bringing a weapon on the scene makes people edgy." It's comforting to me, to know that the person in charge of keeping the peace where I live, believes his job begins with his own body.

"Michelle," he said, when I stopped and waited, at the threshold.

"Hello, Sheriff."

"Come on in." He lowered himself into the chair behind his desk. "How's your folks?"

"Everybody's fine," I said, and sat down in one of the chairs facing his desk. All the furniture in here looked old and well used. There were bulletins and official memos pinned directly to the old paneling on the walls. His desk looked like the ones used by my high school teachers and probably had come out of county storage. There were papers piled here and there on it, but there was a cleared space in the middle, and a framed picture of his wife that, judging by

16

the style of her hairdo and glasses, must have been taken 30 years earlier.

I realized I had been staring at the picture, and I stumbled over something to say, to cover my rudeness. "I was just wondering how you keep a marriage going long enough for a hairstyle to get that out of date."

Then I realized how that must have sounded, and I felt my cheeks burn. I forced myself to look at the Sheriff.

He smiled, then picked up the picture and tilted the frame in the light from the window, to see it better. "You know," he said while he moved the photo back and forth a few inches, to get the focus right, "she wears that exact same style right now."

"Oh no," I said, referring to my rudeness, not his wife's hairstyle, and put my hands on my face as I realized I had just compounded my error.

Sheriff Dolinger laughed out loud. "Been going to the same beautician since they were both 15 years old. I guess Bunny McGlothlin only ever learned one way to cut hair."

"I'm sorry," I whispered. "I didn't mean —"

"But the good thing is, Bunny has always been current in the gossip department, so that makes everything else worth while."

I smiled, he smiled, and everything was okay. "I really would like to know, though," I said, but so quietly the sheriff couldn't hear.

At least, I didn't think he heard me, but after a few seconds' pause, he said, "I don't know what makes a marriage last. Stubborness, maybe. Different things for different folks, for sure."

He looked at me and I had to look away.

"You know, it was different when my generation was getting married. We knew it would be forever; there just wasn't much of a way out of it, once you were in. I guess that made it tough for the ones that really made bad choices. But for the rest of us, it was a comfort."

I still didn't look at him. "Comforting? To be 'stuck'?"

"Well," he said, and leaned back in the swiveling desk chair. "When the hard times came along, we never had to worry, whether he'd stay or she'd stick it out. We never thought much about whether we were making the other one happy, or depended on her making us happy. Heck, we didn't think much about 'happy' at all. We mostly worried about keeping the bills paid and the kids healthy. And your partner was always going to be there, 'happy' or not. It might not have been thrilling, but it sure was comfortable."

I sat and thought about comfort, and the difference between a solid, comfortable marriage, and living a lie.

"Did you really stop by for words of wisdom from an old geezer?"

"Oh! No, of course not," I began, and the sheriff smiled again. "I mean, you know I always like seeing you, but I really do have something to ask you."

"I thought you already did."

"No, not really. I mean, thanks for telling me –"

"You mean, all that was wasted?"

"No, I listened, but I didn't really want you – " I saw his grin and realized I was just making a hole deeper. So I stopped using that particular shovel. "What I really wanted to know was, is it okay with you if I go with ya'll and Sam to Taylor's Ridge on Monday. I want to watch him working." Sheriff Dolinger paused, and looked at me for a few seconds while his mind was clearly elsewhere. Finally, he said, "Did you ask Sam?"

"Well, no. But I don't think he'd care, he's talked to me about dowsing a lot. It's not secret between us."

"He tell you what he'll be looking for, up there?"

"Yes."

Another pause, then, "You get Sam's permission, and I guess it'll be all right."

"Okay. Thanks." I stood up and started towards the door, but turned around to say, "And thanks for the other,

18

too."

"You reckon Phillip would help clean off the old cemetery, next weekend? The men from the church are going to tackle it."

"I... don't know, Don. I'm not sure what Philip's plans are."

The sheriff took another one of those pauses, looking straight at me, and then said, "Well, you tell him, will you?"

"Yeah, I'll tell him. I'll see you on Monday."

I hurried out the door and ran smack into Jimmy Jones' chest. "Whoa!" he said, backing up but not scooting over to make room for me to pass. "You in an awful hurry to get somewhere, ain't ya?"

Jimmy had played football with Phillip, but I'd never known him well. "Sorry," I said. "See you, Jimmy."

I stepped to one side, but Jimmy didn't scoot over. If anything, he might've moved a little toward the center of the hall. I couldn't get by without brushing up against him, which I was not about to do, so I stopped.

"Got to get home and fix a good supper for old man Phillip, I bet."

For some reason, this aggravated me and I heard myself say, "He's the same age as you, Jimmy. You call that old?"

"Well, not so old we can't have a little fun, when the notion strikes."

"You go right on and have your fun, but I've got things to do and places to go," I said, trying to keep it light.

Jimmy stepped aside and I walked on, but he came right behind me. "Speaking of places to go, I hear you're going somewheres with the sheriff on Monday."

"You know you shouldn't listen to other people's conversations," I muttered as I walked through the office. Krystal had left her desk. Jimmy was right on my heels.

"Hey, Michelle, listen," he said, and put his hand on my shoulder. With my hand on the doorknob, I turned around, frowning. He dropped his voice to just above a whisper and spoke before I could say anything. "I know Sam is going up on Taylor's Ridge, to dowse for that body the old man claimed is there. Do you really think Sam could find a body, if it was there and had been in the ground all those months?"

"I *know*," I said clearly, "Mr. Coldiron could find a body, or anything else, no matter how long or how deep it's been buried." I pushed Jimmy's hand off my shoulder, stepped through the doorway, and went home.

Philip Coldiron was two years ahead of me at Highlands High School. He was a fair student and a good football player, from a good family that was solid in the community, not known for anything in particular except for Sam being the go-to man for locating a spring of water.

My own family was not much different. My dad worked for the state Department of Transportation, driving a grader in summer and a snowplow in winter. Mom stayed home and made a big garden every year and we all went to church every Sunday.

I was a little surprised and very pleased when Phil asked me to the prom, his senior year. After that we just kept on dating and everything moved forward at the normal pace, finishing up when we got married.

I was one year into my two-year degree at the community college when Philip came home from Tech without a degree but ready to settle down. We had a nice little church wedding and then I went on and finished my Associate's. Then things began to stall for us.

Philip got home at 5:15 and went to the refrigerator for a beer. I asked him how his work had gone that day, and he said fine. He asked what I'd been into, and I said I'd finished the month's accounts for Janine's. He watched the news on TV until I called him to the table, and even though he would rather have eaten in his recliner, he sat down without complaining.

He never complained, did Philip Samuel Coldiron. He didn't complain about his job at VDOT, where my father was his supervisor. He never complained about not having the Coldiron talent, and I didn't know whether it was from being glad he wouldn't be called on to find underground streams for the road crews or because he had seen the troubles that can come along with it, but whatever his feeling about it, he didn't complain.

He didn't complain about there being no babies in our house and he didn't even complain about me trying to "get into his head," as he called it. He never answered my questions, either.

"You need to eat some salad, too," I said as I put a bowl in front of him. Phil would say he wasn't a picky eater, but there were certain things that didn't touch his lips. Like, almost any vegetables that weren't green beans or potatoes. And for sure, no other cooked vegetables. I fixed salads a lot, but had to encourage him to partake even of those.

I swallowed a bite and said, "I went by your dad's house today."

"How's he?"

"He seemed fine."

Phil grunted in reply, and I thought about how much he and Sam were alike and, at the same time, so different.

"He got a call from the sheriff's department while I was there. They want him to help locate a body, up on Taylor's Ridge."

"Is that right?" Phil chewed on lettuce, then said, "What happen, some hiker fall off a cliff or something?"

Tourists sometimes get lost in our forests. Because the old hills and coves are not dramatic like the Rockies or the Alps, people think they can stroll through them without any care. Every year, one or two get into trouble because they don't respect the weather, the terrain, or the possibilities.

They use their cell phones to call for help when they get tired or lost. It's stretching the rescue squads to the limits of the members' time and ability, not to mention, their charitable feeling for tourists.

"Not exactly." I told him about the deputy's request, but not about the conversation Sam and I had about dowsing. Whether or not Philip regretted not having the ability, I wouldn't rub it in that his father and I had shared a few minutes of real talk about it.

Later, when we got into bed, I asked Phil if he thought it would be okay for me to tag along with Sam when he went up to Taylor's Ridge. "I don't know. Ask Sam, I guess," he said, and turned over on his side. He punched his pillow and settled in and soon he was breathing evenly, deep in the sleep that always seemed to come easily to him. Like a baby. Not that I'd ever had a baby.

I lay awake for a long time, thinking.

I showed up at Sam's house early Monday morning. Once I was there, I asked if I could go up to the Ridge with him. I would like to see him work, I said. I have a thing about watching people work, doing something they're really good at and enjoy. Real work, work that produces results, is one of the good things in life. Someone who's a real master at it - whatever it is, balancing an account to the penny or hammering in nails straight and true - makes it beautiful. I'd seen Sam work at his regular job of carpentering, but I wanted to see him do this work, too. I wanted to see how his body moved, how his face looked when he was reading the "energy." I wanted to understand all of Sam, and be close to him.

He thought about it for a few seconds, and then said, "Yeah." I leaned against the stove while he got his heavy jacket and put his gloves in the pocket. No hat or cap for Sam. He had steel grey hair that he kept strictly trimmed but wore slightly longer than most men his age. It was parted on the side and combed back from a broad forehead that was not divided into tanned and untanned halves, like most men

22

who worked outside.

"Have you ever had on a hat in your life?" I asked, teasing.

Sam glanced at me, raised his eyebrows a little and said, "In Vietnam I wore a helmet or a cap all the time. I said I wouldn't ever again, if I survived."

This, I knew, was a very tender subject, even after all these years. I smiled carefully and said, "Well, here you are."

"And no hat," he said, and I knew we'd passed that trouble without stirring it.

"I never cared for men in hats," I said casually, as we went out the back door. "Who knows what a man is carrying under a hat. It could be extra money or a dead squirrel." Sam laughed. The sound pleased me. I pulled myself into his pickup, and we headed for Taylor's Ridge.

When we got to the pullout near the top of the ridge, we saw that two county cars were already there. Two deputies were standing near the window of one, talking to the man sitting inside it. Sam pulled alongside the cruiser and took his time getting out. I took even longer, giving them time to discuss my presence. By the time I joined them, the question of whether I should or could be there had been settled. Jimmy Jones nodded and Adam, who had graduated from the state police academy and been on the force for about a month, smiled and said, "Hey, Ms Coldiron." I did the books for his mom's diner, and had been seeing him there since he was ten or twelve years old.

Sheriff Dolinger got out of his car and adjusted the handgun on his hip. There was so much leather hanging around his middle, he creaked like a horse in harness when he moved.

"Morning, Michelle. Sam says you want to see your police force in action." The sheriff settled his wide-brimmed hat more securely on his head.

"Well, I'll be glad to report that the people's tax dollars are being well spent."

"You do that." Sheriff of Highlands County is an elected position, and although he hates having to divert his attention from the small robberies, domestic disputes and occasional gory murders that make up the bulk of his work ("There is no anonymous crime in Highlands County," he told me once. "If somebody's going to kill you here, it'll be somebody you know, probably somebody's who's been arguing with you for years, and they're probably going to do a real thorough job of it." I've found this to be generally true.) Sheriff Dolinger is nonetheless aware of potential publicity, good and bad, at all times.

"How does this work?" Adam asked. Everyone looked at Sam.

"I'll just walk through the area where the body's supposed to be. I'll let you know if I think something's there." The men shuffled their feet, and I wondered if, behind their backs or inside their pants pockets, they were crossing their fingers against bad luck. Superstition will rear its ugly head in the most modern person's heart, if nobody's looking.

"What do you want us to do, Sam?" Sheriff Dolinger said.

"Mostly, let me be," Sam leveled a steady gaze on the younger men. "Stay back a little. I need room for the magic wand." Adam swallowed nervously, but Jimmy grinned.

Sam turned to look at the ridge above him. "Did you get a clear idea of where the body should be? Any markers or points?"

"I asked," Sheriff Dolinger said. He moved to stand closer to Sam, facing the same direction. "See that little ledge up there? Beside that big oak, above the laurels?" He raised his right arm, the one next to Sam, and held it steady, pointing up the slope. About halfway up, maybe 1,000 feet, I saw the ledge. "Stansbury said he was sitting on that ledge, or one like it, with his back against the trunk of the tree. He would have been looking east, with the afternoon sun behind him."

The small cliff, as I saw it, jutted out over an undercut.

Thirty or so feet below it, a thicket of rhododendron bushes rolled up to its feet like an ocean swell. From the ledge to the top of the ridge behind it, a distance of perhaps another 500 feet, the slope was much less steep.

"All right," Sam said, and he started up the slope.

He took his time, and it took a long time. He walked all around the face of that part of the ridge, going slowly, sometimes stopping. The other men and I all waited at the bottom, near the cars. We could hear messages going back and forth on the sheriff's radio, and once he reached in and answered a call, then took out his cell phone and called the station. After the first few minutes of silence, Jimmy and Adam relaxed, rested their backsides against the car fenders, used their pocketknives to clean their fingernails or dig splinters out of their hands.

I moved away from the men, watched Sam, and tried to understand what he was doing. If Jimmy or Adam had thought there would be mysterious rituals or magic incantations, they had to have been disappointed. Sam appeared to be looking over the land the way some farmers will do, really looking, seeing how the water was running, how the young crops were growing, how the wind and weather were affecting the plants. Sam looked around a lot, stopping to look up and down the slope, and back and forth across its face. Sometimes, I thought, he was looking for the best place to walk. Other times I thought he might almost have been sniffing the air. He covered the whole face of that section of the slope, centering on the ledge and tall oak tree. It took almost two hours, and then he came back down.

Jimmy and Adam had gotten bored a long time earlier. They were sitting in their car. I think Jimmy had been dozing. The sheriff and I were resting against Sam's pickup. We'd talked, lightly, about his family and the weather, and about the upcoming high school basketball season. His grandson was playing forward, this year, and he had big hopes for a better record than last year's 8--6.

Sheriff Dolinger and I were both watching Sam, and noticed when he started back down the ridge. As Sam neared, our conversation fell off and we waited for him quietly. Sam nodded at us and opened the driver's side door of his truck. He reached inside. Came out with a bottle of water. Food City brand, I noticed, nothing fancy. He took a mouthful, swallowed, asked if we'd like some water.

"No, thanks," I said, and the sheriff said he was "all right."

After Sam had drunk again, Sheriff Dolinger asked, "Well, what do you think?"

Sam seemed to consider, then said, "I think there's something there."

I saw the sheriff's jaw tighten a little, and there was a wait while, evidently, both men thought about things. "Do you know exactly where?" he finally asked.

"East of the ledge, about 250 feet. There is a little gully."

The sheriff looked at the area Sam had described, but the line of sight was blocked by a shoulder of land. "Guess I'd better call the state forensics lab."

"Well... If it won't mess things up too much, I'd like to try again up there, get more specific. Maybe even uncover a little bit of whatever it is." Sam looked at the sheriff with calm sympathy. "We don't want the state people here to disclose the body of a cow some fool was too sorry to bury, do we?"

"You think it's a cow?"

Sam put the water bottle away and reached behind the truck seat. He brought out a cloth bag, bundled around its contents. "No, I don't," he said, simply.

"Didn't think you did." Sheriff Dolinger stepped back and said, "Do what you need to do." Looking up the ridge, the sheriff added, "Sam, we appreciate you."

"Okay," Sam said. Then he looked at me and said, "You want to come along this time?"

26

Yes, yes, yes I did. I nodded, and started walking when Sam did.

He didn't take a direct route up the face of the ridge; he angled back and forth, picking an easier way when there was a choice. He didn't move fast but he walked steadily, and by the time we got to the top of the ridge, I was breathing a little hard. Sam stopped to look at the view. To give me a chance to catch my breath, probably. I noticed he wasn't winded at all.

"Sam," I said, puffing a little extra to show why I asked, "how old are you?"

"Fifty-six," he said, no hesitation.

That's not very old, I thought. Not so very old at all. "I'm 29, and I can barely keep up with you."

"Twenty-nine," he said, and smiled. "That's a whole lot of possibilities. A lot of life in front of you."

"You, too," I said as he turned away. "Twenty, thirty more years, anyway." We stood for a few minutes, looking out across the land. From up there on top of Taylor's Ridge, you can see for miles. Especially at that time of year, when the leaves are off the trees. Roll after roll of hills, lining up, running north to south. Without the fancy dress of summer's leaves, you can see the lay of the land, and the mountains' strength like old bones under a tough hide.

Sam had carried the little sack with him as we'd climbed the hill, and now he began to fold it back, uncover whatever it was in there. I watched him, and felt the touch of sunlight on my face. The cloud cover was breaking up, but the wind was strong and the temperature was near freezing. Somewhere far off, a hunting dog called, telling its master it was on the scent of something rich and wonderful. I had a moment of joy, then, like a knife stab, that I lived in a place of such beauty.

Sam let the sack fall away from its contents: a forked tree branch. He held the branch under his arm for a moment while he folded the sack and stuck it in his jacket pocket, then took the stick in both hands. I went closer to see it better. On its main part, it was as big around as my little finger, and each of the two branches was slightly smaller. The stem of the "Y" was maybe 16 inches long, and the arms were a little shorter. It was smooth and dark, with the bark peeled away and the wood seeming to have been rubbed smooth with care and patience.

"What's that?"

"Dowsing stick. Diviner's rod. Whatever you want to call it. This was my father's. Most dowsers use something like this. It helps pinpoint some things."

"Do you let other people touch it?"

"It's not magic. Or sacred. But I don't like for most people to mess around with my things." Sam held the branch out to me. I took it and looked closely, ran my fingers over its whorls and ridges. I have to admit, I wondered if it would tingle in my hands, or bend towards some magnetic field.

"I oil it once in a while, to keep it from drying out," Sam said. I handed it back. It had been quiet in my hands, smooth and interesting, but not quickened.

We walked off the top of the ridge, towards a shallow gully that ran slightly westward, and down. Sam led the way. I kept close to his side. So I could see what he was going to do.

"There's something over here," he said, speaking softly, almost like he was talking to himself. "Something big, that has a lot of pain in it. But it runs downhill, like a creek, flowing along the bottom of the gully. I wanted the stick to tell me where it begins."

We circled the gully, stopping fifty feet below its beginning at the top of the ridge. I heard the dog again, closer now but still a ridge off. Sam walked over the lip of the gully, down into it, and I clambered down after him. He took one of the arms of the wooden Y in each hand, with the stem held out in front like a compass needle, and started up the gully.

I watched carefully, and at first the stick did not move

at all. Sam appeared to have a good grip on it, his hands turned up, knuckles a few inches apart. He wasn't straining or concentrating only on the stick. He was keeping an eye on it, but he was also watching where he was walking. Otherwise he'd have fallen down, with all the rocks hidden by the foot or more of leaves that had collected in the gully.

After we'd moved ten or twelve feet up the gully, the stick began to move. It vibrated in Sam's hands. I couldn't see how he could be doing that, making it happen. It appeared to be jiggling despite his grip on it. He slowed down, and began moving the stick back and forth, pointing its nose across the width of the gully. Then he'd move a step or two ahead, and check across the gully. He did this again and again, and the movement of the stick would decrease when he aimed it to the right. It was excited by the left-hand side of the gully, and it got more excited the further up we went.

I noticed that Sam was frowning now, and his knuckles looked a little white. "Sam?" I said.

"It's pretty strong," he said. "We're close."

I stepped one step away from Sam, to keep from distracting him. Or maybe from being burned by that energy. We moved another couple of steps up the hill, and then a couple more, and now Sam was breathing hard and the stick, I swear to you, I saw the nose of that stick bending - not jiggling, not the whole thing bouncing, just the end of the stem of the Y - bend up, and up again, and up again until it was almost at a 90-degree angle, and then it sliced down, and Sam let out a little cry, an "Ah!" and the stick flew out of his hands. It shot into the earth in front of Sam like an arrow, burying itself so far in that only a couple inches, just the two ends of the branches, were sticking out of the leaves. I heard it hit home, a slice and a thud, almost together.

Sam was leaning over, his hands, palm to palm, squeezed between his knees. I went to him and leaned over to see his face. "Sam?" I was whispering.

"It's okay," he said. He straightened up, took his

hands out from between his knees, and shook them. I reached out and took Sam's right hand, pulled it towards me so I could see. There was a red streak across his palm, and some little flaps of skin along its edges, like he'd been scratched. The streak was fading as I watched, but the scrape was like a normal wound. Not deep enough to bleed.

I laid my fingertips across the scrape in Sam's palm, and looked at his face. He was looking at me. Sam Coldiron's eyes are not a place for gazing if you are hiding something, so to look at him I had to face some things, be honest about some things I'd avoided in my own head. I was standing there, facing Sam and looking into my own self as well as him, when suddenly Sam's eyes widened and he threw up his head and then he spun around, away from me, pivoting on his left heel. I head a distant "pop" and Sam fell, pulling me down with him, his grip on my hand strong all the way to the ground.

I landed pretty much on top of Sam, and I scrambled to get off, to untangle my feet from his and to get up, but Sam wasn't getting up, and I called him. "Sam, Sam, get up." I called and floundered around in the leaves and the stones kept rolling under my boots and I could hear people coming. I thought it must be Adam and Jimmy, coming to see what was taking so long. I yelled at them to come here, come here, Sam is hurt. Because Sam was hurt, I realized it after I said it. Sam wasn't answering me and there was blood all over the front of his jacket.

But the man who appeared at the edge of the gully, the man with the ball cap and the rifle in his hand, was not Adam or Jimmy, or Sheriff Dolinger, either. I did not know this man at all but I said, "Sam's hurt. Help us, please. Help me get him out of here."

The stranger was breathing hard, keeping one hand over his mouth like he was trying to cover up his panting. Then another man came up and looked at me and Sam, and the two men talked to each other. I didn't hear what they were saying because I was trying to do something that would help Sam. I kept thinking, stop the bleeding. Clear the airways. If he's pale, raise the tail. If he's red, raise the head. Keep the patient warm. All those one-liners I'd learned in health class so long ago. Sam was definitely breathing. That was good, but he was pale. Pale, was that shock or loss of blood? Both?

I tried to think what to do. I looked at Sam's shoulder, and saw a mess of bone and meat and blood, there. Blood was soaking Sam's jacket, down the arm and chest, around to the back. Stop the bleeding, stop the bleeding. I jerked off my coat, pulled off the long-sleeved T-shirt I wore. I folded the body of the shirt into a pad and laid it against Sam's wound, pulled the sleeves around and over to tie it in place. I thought about it for one second, then pulled on those sleeves as hard as I could. I cried out then, for I knew it hurt Sam, but I had to make it tight to stop the bleeding. Stop the bleeding. Sam didn't make a sound.

I tucked my coat around Sam to keep him warm, and then I was grabbed and pulled away. The man, the one with the rifle who had covered his mouth, had his arm around my waist and was dragging me up the side of the gully. I flailed around a little, but I didn't understand what was going on, and I did not fight as much as I could have. When I was out of the gully, the second man put his hand around my wrist and the rifle man took my other wrist and they began pushing and pulling me away, up to the top of the ridge. I kept falling and pulling to go back and I was asking them what was going on and where were we going and what about Sam? But they didn't answer me. They kept pulling and pulling on my wrists, and we kept moving until we came to a car, some beat-up old car, and they put me in the trunk and shut the lid.

It was cold. I was cold, after a while my teeth chattered and then my whole body shook and trembled like an old woman with palsy. Eventually, that stopped and I be-

31

came very sleepy.

Time passed. From the feel of it, we moved, the car and me inside it and I would have said, if I'd been asked, that the two men from the hillside were in the car, too. Once I heard them - or some men, anyway - yelling, so there was more than one other person in the car with me, though they were in the front, warm part. Not with me in the cold trunk.

Also, there was a dog. It probably rode in the back seat, for I could hear it scratching and whining. I could smell it, wet, fusty, stinky. Or maybe it was only the trunk I was smelling, because if I'd thought about it I would have guessed that the dog usually traveled in the trunk. It smelled like it. Or like cat pee. Nasty.

But I didn't much think about the cold or the men or the dog, or even the smell. I thought about Sam, and I was afraid. I was so afraid for Sam's life. There had been so much blood, and an awful vision of bone bits and torn flesh rose up, again and again, in my mind. Sam had survived Vietnam; what a cruel quirk that he should get shot right here, in Highlands County, where people like him and me love the land and the people and feel tied to it all.

I did realize Sam had been shot. It was the shell hitting him that had spun him around, away from me, though I hadn't heard the shot until afterwards. And I did, vaguely, connect the two men with the shooting, and eventually it occurred to me that the men who'd shot Sam had me now, and were hauling me God knew where.

But mostly I thought about Sam, and wanted the warmth of his smile and his eye on my face.

Time passed, but I have no idea how much. The car rattled and shook and we went around curves. I rolled back and forth until I wedged myself, feet against the hump over one wheel, my shoulder and head against the other hump. I hugged myself, bare arms around almost bare body, with only a grey sports bra between me and full frontal nudity, as they warn about in movies. Once the car stopped and I heard the men yelling, arguing, but I wasn't trying to understand what they were saying. Sam, Sam, I was thinking. Come and get me.

That was crazy, because Sam was hurt. He might have been in worse shape than me.

Car doors slammed and vibrated my dog-smelling cell, and when the car engine started and the car backed up, exhaust fumes flowed in like dirty water and I began to drown in this river. But when the car started moving forward, the flood of exhaust in my trunk was drained away, replaced by fresher, colder air blowing in through a hundred cracks and holes.

Finally, the car stopped again, and I slept, deeply, without dreams. When I was able to think again, I was being pulled from the car and there were more voices. One of them was a woman's.

"My God, where's her clothes? Ya'll been doing her?"

"No, we ain't been doing her. We been trying to get rid of her."

"Well, you ain't had much luck, have you?"

"Shit, Nadine, what're we gonna do? We got to get rid of her."

"Hey, don't ask me, this is your problem. But you'd better get her away from here. The police will be looking for her, you can bet on that, and we do not want any police anywhere near here. Get rid of her, Jeremy."

I couldn't make sense of anything that I heard, and very little that I felt. Sleep was all I wanted. It was like sleep was a big, warm quilt that I could pull around me and shut out any bad thoughts or pain. Once out of the trunk, I dropped to the ground.

"Nadine," said one of the voices. He was begging, wheedling. "Let us stay here for a while, 'til we get this figured out. Come on Baby, you know me and you are a good thing, and we'll just come up with a way to get rid of her, and then we can pack up and go, if we want to."

"I don't want to go anywhere. I'm tired of being on the move. We can stay here if you don't bring. the. cops. down. on us." Nadine had punctuated her sentence with what sounded like good, hard slaps.

"Hey! Cut it out, bitch!"

"Oh yeah?" Slap, slap. "You dumbass. What did you think you were doing, anyway? Why'd you bring her in the first place?"

"A hostage," said a different male voice. Some part of me was listening, but it all seemed to be happening a long way away. We could use her as a hostage, and make the police back off. If we'd needed to. Besides, she and that old guy found the body.

That old guy, I thought. That was... Sam. Who was not really so very old.

Sam. I am cold, Sam.

I must've said his name, or something like it. They all quieted down, and somebody grabbed my arm, pulled me up.

"Hey," he said, the man who hadn't begged the woman to let them stay. "Wake up. We need to talk to you." He shook my arm and pulled at me, and finally someone slapped me. I pushed my eyes open and looked into the woman's face, a not-pretty face, with dirty hair hanging lank and dull around it, and snot gathering at each nostril, and burnt-looking eyes.

No, not a pretty face, and she saw that in my eyes, I guess, because she drew back her left fist and slammed it into my cheekbone. Then she leaned down to where I was lying on the ground, and when she spoke, I saw the rotten stubs of her teeth.

"You'll get yours," she said.

They put me in the trunk again, and the pain in my cheek kept me awake for a while. The time I was lying in the pissy-smelling trunk, when the car wasn't moving and the dark oblivion of sleep was a drug I couldn't score, when I was facing the facts of my situation, that was a bad time. I didn't think much about the possibility of being rescued, and I didn't have to try to think about escaping. There was no out. I was just there.

Finally someone got in the front of the car, the transmission ground reluctantly into gear, and we started moving. Eventually, with movement, sleep came, and when the car stopped and someone came to the rear and opened the trunk, I was even more groggy and stiff than before. I couldn't walk. Dragging me was so much trouble, they finally carried me, one holding my arms and the other my legs, to a place they had gotten ready. It was nighttime, I think.

They took me to a place. They dropped me in. I remember a door, a wooden door, shutting. I remember that very distinctly, that sound, and I knew, even then, when I was muddled and confused, what it was. I heard the rattle and knock of dirt and stone falling on the door, too, but I wasn't aware of what that meant. I didn't figure it out for a long time.

This really wasn't the worst part. It wasn't. Everybody thinks it must be, that being shut up in an old cellar under the ground, in the dark and without any idea that you'd ever get out, would be horrible. It *was* horrible, but it wasn't worse than that period in the trunk, when it was all settling into my mind. And I was so cold, in the trunk, when I was awake. At least under ground, it was warmer. One of the men, Jeremy, dropped his jacket into the hole with me. It was because he believed the jacket would smell like me, he said. Jeremy and the other man argued about it. Other Man said it would connect them with the body, if it was ever found, but Jeremy (It must have been his dog who rode with us from Taylor's Ridge to the house.) said the body - mine, I realized later - wouldn't ever be found, if the dogs couldn't track them to the site. He wasn't about to keep on wearing a jacket that smelled like the victim (me again, when I thought about it), he said, and he threw the jacket into the cellar. It fell right on top of me. After a while, I put it on.

35

Eventually, hunger came to visit, but thirst came much quicker and was a much meaner guest. Thirst drove me to lick the dirt walls, but there was not much moisture there, except once, when it rained. I don't know where the air came from. It was stuffy in there, but not suffocating. Someone said there was an old vent, towards the back, mostly blocked with dirt and trash.

In one way, the darkness was a blessing. I think if I'd been able to see the cellar walls, had had the undeniable, visual truth of how small my prison was, I wouldn't have been able to take it. In the dark, you can imagine all kinds of things, places and doorways and passages and space. Just space.

And people. In the dark in the cellar, I talked to a lot of people. Sam came to visit, and my grandmother who'd been dead for six years. I asked her about a lot of things, and if it was just a hallucination, if all her answers really came out of my own head, I wish I could've learned them sooner, without being buried alive.

I got weak. Sleep came more and more often, and restlessness, that had caused me to walk round and round and beat on the walls and try to dig with my hands and my boot--I took one off and tried to rip the upper from the sole, so I could use the sole for a shovel, but these were fine boots, and the parts would not part from themselves even to help a poor stranded female--the restlessness left me.

At one point in this final peacefulness, an idea floated up into my consciousness like a bubble rising: if Sam had been alive, he might have found me. With his family gift of dowsing, with his ability both rare and universal of finding and following the energy of water or of lost things held with emotion, if he had loved me as I had begun to believe I loved him, Sam Coldiron might have saved me from the grave. But Sam, I decided, wouldn't come. He must have died.

Then a great weight was on my chest, and a brilliant light burned my eyes. Air, warm and soft and smelling like apple blossoms, settled on my face and my spirit began to rise to meet it. I thought that death, after all, was not frightening or dark as life had become for me.

But then I felt something different. I was shaken and pulled and I heard someone saying my name. I couldn't raise my head or open my eyes, but inside me, something was stirring. "Michelle, Michelle, Michelle," I heard, and at last, at long last, I turned toward the one who called me to him. He'd found me with his rare and nearly universal gift that had only needed need to be awakened.

I answered by whispering his name, "Phillip."

Joe Martin

Joe Martin had a gift. He knew that most people would have been frightened by or at least felt uncomfortable with it, but Joe had found it to be serviceable to his profession. Joe was a certified mortician and funeral director, and he could tell if someone was going to die.

It was only people he actually touched, and he usually only "caught it" if the death was going to happen relatively soon – within a few months. It had started as just a feeling that would come into his awareness when he touched certain people. At first, he hadn't even realized what it meant. As years had gone by, though, and perhaps because he'd become so aware of the certainty of death coming for all of us, and as he became ever more desirous of ways to smooth the process of passing, Joe had begun to pay attention to and understand these feelings. With a little forewarning, plans could be set, equipment would be readied, materials could be acquired; many ways to help the deceased ease out of life and the bereaved be reconciled to their loss could be prepared.

When Joe shook Mrs. Johnson's hand after her mother's funeral, he made a quick mental calculation: She's not a tall woman, no, not really tall. Average height, or maybe even a little below. A little below average height, but very wide. Oh my yes, definitely wide. Three-fifty, maybe even three-sixty, and that means a special order, and special orders are so very expensive. Joe decided he would get with the casket company today, telling them he would need an extra-wide casket, probably a wooden one, and that he'd need it delivered in about... a month. He wished Mrs. Johnson would be as forward-thinking and thoughtful as her mother had been. Now there had been a real lady, a woman who knew how to prepare and make things easier for her children as well as to assure that things went as she wanted them to. Goodness knows, young people these days often didn't have a clue. They just didn't have a clue.

Although Joe Martin liked to tell people that he had been in the funeral business for "more than 50 years," the truth was he'd actually been in the business for 70 years. These numbers were in his mind because they'd had a viewing on his birthday. He'd realized it was his birthday when he'd set up the guest register and written the date on the first line (The public was so funny about that; if the first person to sign failed to write in the date, no one else would, either. Maybe they wouldn't know what the date was, or they weren't sure if they were supposed to, but for whatever reason, there it would be, a long wavering column of emptiness where the dates should be. Joe Martin was bothered by wavering and by empty spaces where things should be but weren't, so he found a way to keep the guest books neat and tidy. He always went ahead and wrote in the date for the first arrival.) and it had struck him: exactly 70 years ago, on his sixteenth birthday, he'd assisted at his first funeral.

That deceased had been one of the patriarchs of the county, yes, a leading figure in church and business, and Joe's employer and the man from whom he would later buy the business, Mr. R. Richard Blevins, had known that the funeral would be lengthy and large. So even though Joe had only shaken hands with Mr. Blevins the week before, agreeing to help dig graves and drive trucks for the outdoor work, Mr. Blevins had told Joe to be properly dressed and in the parking lot by 8:00 that morning. And he'd given Joe five dollars to buy a suit; he'd never owned one before that time.

As he walked down the aisle of the Green Parlour, checking to make sure no memorial programs had been left in the seats, no Kleenex or gum wrappers overlooked by the cleaning crew, Joe recalled that first funeral.

How different things had been, in those days! Why, even though many people had found someone with a car with whom they could catch a ride, there were still several horse-and-buggy arrivals needing direction. Nineteen and thirty-four, it was, and here in this county, some people from out in the hinterlands had still come to town in horse and buggy.

And everybody had to come to that funeral.

While the other assistant pointed the way for the trucks and cars to line up, down the center of the grassy lot, I had to stand at the far end of the line, directing people to "Put 'er there" or to "Back 'er up a little," and for those who arrived in buggies to pull under the big oak trees over on the east side of the lot, where the horses or mules could wait in the shade.

In those days, funerals were day-long events. There would have been three or four preachers. Sometimes women passed out from the heat and exhaustion, and men gathered in the back of the church, passing their flat bottles back and forth. Oh yes.

Although Joe regretted some of the things that had changed about the funeral tradition over the years, there were many that he did not miss.

Joe reached the front of the Parlour, and turned to give it a final check. Everything was in order. He turned off the lights – no need to waste money lighting areas where there were no people -- and exited through the double doors that led into the hallway. He stepped quietly and at moderate speed down the nice, thick but sturdy carpet, past the doors to the other parlours and the stairway down to the main floor, and entered his private office. He called the casket company and placed an order for an extra-large oak casket, lined in silver blue, to be delivered in four weeks.

"You the man to see about a funeral?"

The person who stood in front of Joe at the front desk was young, probably in his early twenties, and was dressed in jeans, a dark T-shirt with some kind of design printed across the chest, and an unbuttoned flannel shirt on top of it. He had on heavy work boots which were, Joe was in no doubt of it, depositing little clots of dried mud on the carpet, even as Joe watched.

Nevertheless, every person deserved the respect due to the bereaved, whether of the highest social standing or the lowest. And these days, it was sometimes hard to tell which was which.

Joe stood and walked around the desk. He made an instantaneous decision about whether to stick out his hand for this young man to shake. Some people needed a human touch and some people shied away from it. This boy seemed of the latter variety, so Joe stopped at a medium-range distance and said, "I'm Joe Martin. I own and operate Hometown Funeral Services, and have for 50 years. How can I be of service to you today?"

"I need to arrange for a funeral."

The man seemed unsure whether to offer an explanation or demand an estimate. Joe made a slight turn and lifted one hand towards the Little Conference Room, to the left of the front desk. "Why don't we go where we can sit down?" Joe lifted his other hand to shepherd the fellow towards the room, and briefly touched his back. *No sign*, he thought. *This boy has a long life ahead of him.*

The Little Conference Room (as distinct from the

Front Conference Room) was decorated in blue and cream, with homey touches to make people feel at ease. There were little framed cross-stitches, done by Joe's wife Emmaline, expressing sweet sentiments such as "Home, Sweet Home" and "Resting in Hope." The small Early American couch – just big enough for two – was centered against the wall furthest from the desk, and there was a rocking chair with matching cushions in the corner. The two straight chairs in front of the desk were from the suite Emmaline used in their own, personal breakfast nook: Early American maple, with honey blond finish. There were Kleenex boxes, with white tissues aloft, positioned discretely around the room. Very clean, nice, but not intimidating; no, not intimidating.

Joe took his seat behind the desk. "Now, have you suffered a recent loss, or are you planning ahead?"

The young man seemed a bit puzzled. "Granny died," he finally said.

"I am so sorry to hear it. Please sit down." While the man sat, pulling the chair back a little and adjusting his behind in it, Joe opened a drawer (soundlessly; he insisted that all the drawers in the building be carefully maintained and screech-less) and lifted out a pre-stacked pile of papers and forms. He knew very well that there had been only two deaths in the local hospital in the past 24 hours, one a middle-aged man who had been crushed when his tractor rolled over him, and the other an elderly woman who'd not suffered long from an undiagnosed cancer. The man's body would almost certainly go to Joe's competition in the county seat, since he was a relative newcomer to the area and his family would go to the most modern-appearing business. The other was likely this young man's grandmother, although there was no ruling out a home death or the return of someone who'd moved to be with family, years ago. "And who was your grandmother?" Joe was careful to keep his voice smooth, quiet, solicitous but not sticky.

"Aileen McKinney."

McKinney, McKinney. While selecting a pen from the holder placed in the right-hand corner of the desk, and taking the first form from the pile and pulling it into careful position in front of him, Joe considered who the departed had been in life, and who her connections were, and what communities she had been a member of. All these things would help him offer the best, most appropriate, service to Aileen McKinney's survivors. "Would that be, Mrs. McKinney, from the Pine Branch McKinneys?"

"Yeah." The man was settled in the chair; he leaned back a little when Joe mentioned Pine Branch. He knew now that Joe would steer him right.

"And you are Mrs. McKinney's grandson?"

"Yeah. Jack's son."

"Oh yes. If I remember correctly, your father worked for Halsey Lumber?" The phone on the desk rang, softly, but Joe ignored it; it would only ring twice before the answering machine picked up. His rule was, the person you are looking at is more important than the person on the phone.

"Yeah, till he died, four year ago. I work there now."

Joe thought for a second and recalled that Jack McKinney had died on the job, from a heart attack. Fell over while operating a crane, lifting logs onto a big conveyor. Joe's assistants had gone to the site and transported the body first to the hospital, where it was autopsied, and then back to the business to be embalmed. The funeral had been held at the Pine Branch church, with burial following in the family cemetery – a long drive through a sloping hayfield. "I've always heard that Halsey's is a good place to work." Joe knew he was altering his speech, dropping into patterns and vocabulary that were his from childhood but that were usually obliterated by his profession. He didn't do it deliberately, but he knew it happened; he believed it was good for the work, that it made people feel comfortable talking to him. Because it was his own, honest, native tongue, and the style he thought of as his "formal" was just as genuine and learned from the

44

profession he'd practiced for so long, he felt that switching to suit the customer was not a trick he did to get more business, but part of the package of care and support he offered.

"Pretty good. They have good benefits, but we get laid off some." The boy lifted the cap on his head and replaced it, adjusting its bill slightly to the right: a sign of his lessening tension.

"I am so sorry to hear that Ms Aileen has passed," Joe said, bringing them back to the business at hand. "Did she leave instructions...?"

"No..." The boy straightened in the chair, which told Joe this was a sticky subject. "Well, you know, Granny told some of us she wanted to be buried up there close to Grandpa and Daddy, but that's all she said about it."

"I see," Joe murmured.

"Aunt Ruth and some of them, they think she should be cremated ("cre-mated," the boy said, with emphasis on the first syllable) or something. They think they ain't no use of trying to have a service in the church, or have people come to the house, or anything like that."

"I understand," Joe said gently. He did understand. When people moved away from the area and they saw new ways of doing things, got established in a new community, they didn't see the point of doing things the old-fashioned way. He knew, too, that Pine Branch was Primitive Baptist, and people who move out of the area soon lost sight of the old church traditions, their meaning and comfort. They quickly lost respect for the men who worked alongside their neighbors six days a week and put on ill-fitting suits and preached on Sundays. They weren't moved by sermons based on individual interpretations of King James texts. People got to where they were embarrassed by their old church's hypnotic cadences and atonal, unaccompanied hymns.

Joe heard the bells over the front door jingle. He looked over at the boy in the ball cap. "These situations can be rough, but maybe we can work together to satisfy everyone's requirements."

"I don't see how," he said gruffly. "Aunt Ruth's boy, Jimmy –"

"What's your name, son?" Joe interrupted, aware that the person who had come in the front door would wait for only a few seconds, and then he (or she) would start walking the halls to find a living human being to talk to. Funeral parlours did that to most people, made them think they would bump into a ghost if left alone a single minute.

"Mack. But Jimmy --"

"Mack, if you'll excuse me for just a moment, I need to tend to someone up front. But I'll be right back. You just relax here, try to relax and rest for a few minutes." Joe stood up and paced carefully through the door, then hurried up the hall towards the front desk. Just as he came within sight, Mrs. Johnson turned around to face him, clearly about to start wandering.

"Mrs. Johnson," Joe said mildly. "Can I help you?"

"Mr. Martin, I forgot my mama's pearls," she said, a little breathless.

Joe took a moment, tilted his head a few degrees. "Your mother was wearing her pearl necklace while she was here. I'm sure of it."

"Oh yes, I know she had them *on*," she said. She looked around and Joe automatically stepped around to the foyer and started to pick up the nice wooden chair with the faux-tapestry-covered seat. He hesitated, then walked quickly through a doorway and returned with a sturdy office chair, and placed it close to Mrs. Johnson.

"Please, have a seat," he said. She was already on her way onto it.

"Thanks. Oh, people commented on that necklace and how nice it looked. People said she looked so pretty. Mr. Martin, you did an excellent job with Mama."

"Thank you."

"Her hair and makeup were really nice, not too much,

you know? I always hate it when dead people look like Barbie dolls, too much makeup and the wrong color lipstick."

"Yes." Joe was pleased; he usually did the deceased's hair himself, and applied any makeup that might be necessary. That was his secret: he felt strongly that it was not necessary to use makeup on every body, and rarely did it look best to use very much. Just a touch, that was all. You didn't want a loved one to look like a ghost, but you didn't want them to look as Mrs. Johnson said, like a plastic doll. Of course, you always had to keep the family's wishes in mind.

"And Mama would have been pleased. She was always a little prissy, you know, and wanted to look good whenever she was out in public."

"Yes," Joe inserted into the flow, "but now I –"

"And the necklace was a nice touch, wadn't it?"

"Yes. I'm afraid I –"

"Well, that's what I came here for. Because I forgot to pick up that necklace."

Joe froze in place.

"You know, that necklace was a gift from my daddy. My real daddy, I mean. He died in the war, you know. They got married and he was shipped out, and then Mama found out she was pregnant with me. He got to come home – from some kind of training, I guess – when I was two months old. There are pictures of him holding me, but of course I don't remember it, and then he was killed just a few months later. He bought that necklace while he was overseas somewhere. Japan, I guess. Sent it home and it got here after Mama got word that he'd been killed."

"It was a fine necklace," Joe said, faintly.

"It was always supposed to be mine, but Mama wore it a lot more than me. I mean, it wouldn't even go round my neck, after I put on so much weight."

"Could have been altered..." Joe muttered, but Mrs. Johnson rolled on.

"You know, I've been in such a state, I couldn't remember anything. It's been a God's true wonder that I haven't walked out of the house without my underwear or something. And you know, I haven't felt so good either, lately. Of course, I guess it's because of Mama being sick and in the hospital and there was nobody to help make any of the decisions."

Joe allowed himself to lean against the Front Desk. "Your son," he inserted quietly.

"Well, you know my son is living in Germany now, and he has a life of his own and he didn't have time to return all my calls, and that's so expensive, anyway. Of course, he was here for the funeral. Did you get to meet him?"

"No, I don't believe I had the pleasure."

"He's the last one of us, the last one of either my late husband's or my family's line. I think that's sad, don't you? There'll be no more Johnsons and no more Baileys, either, at least, none of direct lineage."

"Perhaps he'll have children to carry on the name," Joe said, mesmerized in spite of himself.

"Oh no, Michael is *gay*, Mr. Martin, there's no chance of a grandchild for me. I know you do hear of gay couples adopting children these days, but that's not the same, is it? The blood connection wouldn't be there."

Joe wasn't particularly shocked by Mrs. Johnson's news about her son's situation, or that she'd told him about it. In his business, you found out many, many secrets and besides, being what they used to call "funny" wasn't such a big deal, anymore. But thinking about sons reminded Joe of his client still waiting in the Little Conference Room.

Although his mind was still stalled on the idea that a pearl necklace might have been... not attended to... Joe straightened and said, "Mrs. Johnson, I have to meet with another client at this moment. I have to --"

"Oh, I didn't know there was somebody else here. Who died?"

This, too, was part of the job: news of deaths, even

more than news of births, must be circulated to family, friends, neighbors, even people whose connection to the deceased was just that they had gone to school together fifty years ago. Folks needed to know so they could offer their sympathy, carry in food, share memories. Support, is what it all adds up to, Joe thought. He answered Mrs. Johnson, "Mrs. Aileen McKinney, from Pine Branch."

"Pine Branch... Well, I don't believe I know them."

"Thank you for coming by today, Mrs. Johnson," Joe said, and he reached for Mrs. Johnson's hand.

Mrs. Johnson did not start the process of hoisting herself from the chair. "But," she said, looking up at Joe and taking a stern grip on her handbag, "I haven't gotten my pearl necklace."

Just then, Joe became aware of the soft swish of heavy boots on the carpet, and he turned to see Mack McKinney in the doorway. "Uh, Mr. Martin?" Mack said.

"Mr. McKinney, I was just on my way to you. We'll finish our talk now." Joe turned to Mrs. Johnson and took her hand, lifting it from the purse and grasping it firmly. "Goodbye, Mrs. Johnson. I'll be in touch very soon, and we can take care of these details. Thank you for coming in today." He turned quickly but smoothly, slipped to Mack McKinney's side, and ushered the boy back down the hallway to the LCR. Never, never let a civilian wander around in a mortuary; they are so very likely to stumble into situations that would be upsetting to those not in the profession.

On top of the worry about the pearl necklace, Joe had suffered another shock: Mrs. Johnson's death was coming much sooner than he'd thought. Her handshake had told him. Joe would have to adjust his plans and call the casket company again.

Back in the conference room, Mack settled into the chair and Joe returned to the swivel chair behind the desk. (Swivel, but not, ever, rolling.) "Now, let's see," he began. "Are you the person who will be responsible for the arrangements?" He held the good black pen ready, above the form, waiting.

"Well," Mack said, and leaned forward, "see, that's the problem, right there."

Joe laid the pen down carefully, so it did not make a sound, and crossed his wrists on the desk. "Is there someone, a responsible party, coming in from some distance?" Joe hoped against hope that this was the issue.

"No, it's just..." Mack shifted in his chair, and reached up to adjust his cap, settling it so the bill faced straight out in front. "See, no offense to Aunt Ruth or anybody, but it's like, they don't live here any more, and they don't know how we do things. And Granny, you know, she was pretty old-fashioned."

"I see," Joe said softly.

"You know, I wouldn't cause a breakup in the family for nothing, not if I could help it," Mack looked around the room, probably wishing for a way out. "I mean, hell, maybe Aunt Ruth is right, and nobody would come to a wake at the house. Maybe we should have uh, uh, what do you call it, a memorial service, right here at the chapel, and let it go at that."

"Many people do choose to have a service here," Joe stated calmly.

"Well." Mack settled back in his chair, and look directly at Joe. "But I just keep thinking, that's not what Granny woulda wanted."

Joe sat, and waited.

"Granny was, she was like, older than her years, in some ways. I mean, she wasn't feeble or anything. She wasn't even sick til just a couple of weeks before she died. But she liked doing things the old way. She kept on in that house that Grandpa built when they were first married, and she cooked every bite of food in a big old wood cookstove. And she always wore dresses, you know? Never did give in to wearing pants. And aprons, a clean one every day. Never had much

50

use for a television. And, and... She was a sweet old woman."
Mack bent his head to hide tears that slid from the corners of
his eyes.

"Mr. McKinney," Joe said, "I'm going to ask you a
question that you have to believe has nothing to do with my
interests, my business interests. Okay?"

Mack didn't respond, and Joe went on.

"Mr. McKinney, who is going to take financial respon-
sibility for your grandmother's final disposition?"

Mack looked up and sniffed, a good, solid snort, not
a weak little sniffle. He looked Joe full in the face for a long
moment. "Granny has a little money put away for the pur-
pose. But I got a feeling it won't be enough. If there's more
owed than there is money to pay for it, I guess I'll sign on for
it, though I don't have it right on hand."

"I asked, Mr. McKinney, because it has always been
my policy that the ones who bear the financial responsibil-
ity, should have the most say in how things are done. In this
case, you know the general shape of your grandmother's
wishes, and she left funds to cover at least some of that. It
seems to me like that's pretty clear. Do you agree?"

"Yes."

"Now, it may seem indelicate of me, but I need to ask
how much money she left. We can decide what is the most
important of the expenses, and what else we want to have.
We can get things petty well settled, and then, if you want,
you can let others of the family say a thing or two, and then
we'll proceed. All right?"

"All right," Mack said, and breathed deeply.

Joe and Mack talked for nearly an hour, comparing
the money Mrs. McKinney had stashed in a tin box on her
kitchen shelf with what Mack had heard her say about funerals and such, and in the end, things fell fairly neatly into
place. Yes, there would be a funeral service preached at her
church, and a nice but not flashy wooden casket, and there
were grandsons and nephews enough to carry the casket

up to the old cemetery and yes, Joe's assistants would have everything ready and in place. The day and time had been settled, and the preachers had been glad to be asked to preside. Mrs. McKinney's money would cover all but $425, and Mack took a coupon book to help him remember to pay it off in $35 installments (thirteen months), no interest.

Joe escorted Mack McKinney to the front door and just as he was shaking Mack's hand goodbye, he heard a slight creaking from above. He waited until Mack was through the door and two steps away, and then turned to look up at the ceiling over his head. There was nothing obvious to show why the ceiling should be creaking, but Joe realized it was not the ceiling, but the second-story floor that rested upon it, that was making the noise. Someone was walking around in the Green Parlour.

Joe hurried down the dim hallway and up the stairs. Halfway up, he could see that the lights were on in the Green Parlour, and he realized that someone was standing at the top of the stairs, waiting for him. Before he could positively identify the back-lit figure, Mrs. Johnson's voice floated down to him. "There you are. You know, after we talked I ran an errand and then, as I was heading towards home, I thought, maybe that necklace got dropped in the funeral home. Just slipped out, some time. So I drove around to the upper lot and the doors were unlocked, so I came on in. I've been looking around, but I haven't seen a sign of it."

"No. The Parlour has been cleaned." Joe ascended two more steps, then stopped, still several steps below Mrs. Johnson. From that position, her bulk loomed suffocatingly over him.

"Well, Mr. Martin, you know I'm getting worried about that pearl necklace."

"I don't recall having a conversation with you about the necklace, during our discussions of arrangements," he said mildly.

"Oh no, I gave it to your assistant, that Bill man, and

I told him I wanted it put on her. And I reminded him to be sure to take it off, too. We did not want it to go to the crematorium with Mama!"

"Of course not." Joe, feeling suddenly a little weak, put his hand on the handrail.

"I mean," Mrs. Johnson said, actually raising her voice. Joe Martin hated raised voices, especially in his place of business, where it was so important to maintain a sense of calm and orderliness. People have to have faith in their undertakers! "I mean, it was not supposed to be burned up with her! It was a memento of my father! It was worth hundreds, maybe even thousands!"

"Mrs. Johnson, please."

"Don't 'please' me, I want my necklace!"

"I'm sure it will turn up –"

"Turn up! Why isn't it where it's supposed to be, Mr. Martin? That's what I'd like to know. Seems to me that either somebody has stolen my pearl necklace, stolen it right off my dead mother's neck, or that it's been burnt up in a crematorium furnace and there's nothing left of it but ashes. Oh, boo hoo."

In all Joe Martin's time of attending ladies in distress, he had never heard another utter those actual words, the cries of storybook babies. He climbed three more steps so that he was on the hall floor, standing beside the sobbing Mrs. Johnson, and reached to pat her round shoulder. But with his hand only an inch from actual contact, Joe Martin was struck into immobility. It was as though there was a halo of energy around Mrs. Johnson, that buzzed inaudibly and was reaching an unbearable pitch so that something was going to have to happen right now or there would be an explosion, and Joe realized what it was, knew that Mrs. Johnson was dying NOW –

"Mr. Martin?" called a voice from below.

Mrs. Johnson shrieked, emitting another storybook cry, this one the short, high-pitched "eek!" of a cartoon lady seeing a mouse, and she tried to step back, away from the eerie voice rising from the darkness at the foot of the stairs. Something twisted, something collapsed, something overcorrected. She fell.

Joe tried to catch her, but the more than three hundred pounds were far too much for him to hold. She thudded down all the stairs, and it seemed to Joe that at each stair, there was a separate and distinct crunch. Some came with dull cracking sounds. Finally, there was a dreadful silence.

"Mr. Martin?" came a shaky whisper from below.

"Yes?" Joe answered, not sure, at that moment, who or what might be seeking him.

"It's me, Mack. McKinney. I think she's dead."

Joe took a moment to breathe and swallow. "I imagine so," he finally agreed.

"Shit," Mack said, but he probably meant it only for himself.

Still, "Yes, probably so," Joe said. They stayed in place, each trying to understand what had just happened and what some of the consequences might be, and what had to be done now. Finally, following his own train of thought, Mack remembered something.

"I wanted to tell you something," he said.

"Okay," Joe answered.

"I answered your phone."

"My phone?"

"When you were out there talking to that woman – I mean, it was this woman, wasn't it?"

"Yes."

There was a little pause then, as if Mack was contemplating the mystery of connections and near-misses. "Well, while you were out there, your phone rang and I answered it."

"Okay."

"But I forgot to give you the message."

"Oh. Was it important?"

"Well, I don't really know. But when I remembered, I come back in to tell you. In case, you know, it was important."

"Okay. Thank you."

"Well. The message was, it was somebody named Bill, and he said to tell you the necklace is in an envelope in the bottom drawer of the front desk."

There was another silence then, that lasted while the men each drew three or four breaths. Then Joe Martin said, "Mr. McKinney, do you have any very important things you have to do this afternoon? Because I think I will need you to be here when the police ask some questions."

An Insurance Nightmare

It was an insurance nightmare, is what it was. The Rescue Squad covered Jimmy Gleason's concussion, and the Bedsaul's homeowner's covered the damage to their house, what wasn't under the deductible, but I never did hear who paid for Bill's arm. I guess Bill and Velma paid for a new snake out of their own pocket.

I have said all along that it was the snake that was the real culprit, but I have heard people blame it on the dog, or on the little boy, and even on the teacher. Some on the Rescue Squad have even tried to make out like it was Fred Clodfelter's fault, but I say it was a matter of instinct, to react like that. Some people are just made that way, to run from a snake, and nobody ought to hold it against Fred. I still say that the rail on the gurney shouldn't have had a space wide enough for Bill's arm to get caught in, and there is some liability there on the part of the manufacturer. But nobody listens to me.

By the last day of school, Miss Krystal Hampton, the first grade teacher at Goodview Elementary School, still had not found a summer home for Barkley, the two-foot long black snake that had lived the whole school year in the glass tank in the corner of the classroom. There was sand in the bottom of the tank, and a good-sized rock and a piece of driftwood for Barkley to climb up on when he took the notion, and all in all, Barkley had had a pretty good winter. Thanks to climate-controlled conditions, he had not even been inclined to go into the long sleep of winter hibernation.

On special days the children were allowed to hold Barkley, and he took this with reasonably good grace, since Miss Hampton instructed each and every child in the proper way to hold him so none of his ribs was crushed and pieces of him didn't dangle or droop. Also, she kept the screen firmly locked over the top of the tank while Barkley was shedding his skin. Some things should be done by each person alone by himself, Miss Hampton said. The students were agreeable.

But now here it was, the last day of school, and not one friend had agreed to babysit Barkley, even just for the summer. Miss Hampton couldn't take the snake home with her, because she was planning to take a six-week camping trip to the Rockies with her boyfriend Lewis, during which trip she would have enough trouble convincing Lewis that turning jockey shorts inside out did not equal fresh underwear. She knew there would definitely be no energy for maintaining a snake in an aquarium as well as Lewis in the wild.

She had asked each of the teachers in her wing of Goodview to temporarily adopt Barkley, but even with her assurances that he only had to be fed once a week, those feedings did consist of live mice. If a snake in the house is just plain scary to some people, adding a regular deposit of live mice into the serpent's den (so to speak) only adds disgust to the fear. One woman who has thirty-two years' experience teaching second-graders and has, as you will understand, seen pretty much everything, said the only thing she could image that was worse than keeping a snake in her house was bringing live mice in for the snake's amusement.

No thank you very much.

So on the last day of school, in some desperation, Miss Hampton asked if any of the students wanted to take Barkley home with them for the summer. Every grubby little hand in the classroom shot up, and a lottery had to be instituted, and when Billy Bedsaul's name was drawn, Miss Hampton drew a sigh of relief and sent him to the office with instructions to call his momma and ask her if it was all right to bring Barkley home with him.

In a reasonable amount of time Billy came back and reported that his momma had said okay, and Miss Hampton had no reason to think it was suspicious. It was her first year of teaching.

Later on we found out from Velma that what Little Billy called and asked was if it would be okay for Barkley to come home from school with him. Velma thought he was asking to bring home one of the other little boys, and she said it would be fine if they would be quiet when they got in, because Billy's daddy would be sleeping because he'd worked a third shift and wouldn't be getting up till 4:30 or 5.

Billy promised to be quiet, and that was that. See, Velma and Bill were married for about twelve years before Velma finally got pregnant. They had already given up hope, and when that little boy was born, they figured it was their one shot at parenthood. Velma set her mind on being the best mother in the world. She quit her job at the Six and Seven Dress Shoppe and stayed home and kept house and baked cookies and read a lot of Little Golden Books to the boy and encouraged Little Billy to play well with others, including bringing them home with him whenever the opportunity arose.

Little Billy seemed to have gotten the best of both his parents. He got the smarts of the Gunnels. Velma's people were always quick but sometimes went astray. That's what Preacher Snap said, when Velma's Uncle Gilmer was sent to the regional jail for 3 to 5 for grand theft auto. Old Gilmer just went a little astray, and he went quick, in somebody else's car.

So the kid got Gunnel smarts but he also got his daddy's folks'es sweetness. They are the kind of people who are quiet and easy, who work hard but not hard enough to get ahead of their neighbors. They never feud, are never nominated for Volunteer of the Year, but they go to every fund-raising dinner and put $5 in the collection plate every Sunday.

When Billy got off the school bus that afternoon, he had Barkley in his lunch box and Barkley's aquarium in his backpack. It made the pack look huge, but it wasn't all that heavy, and by putting the snake in the lunch box Billy didn't have to keep the aquarium upright and lidded, and have all the kids on the bus poking and prodding at the snake. So the bus driver didn't notice anything unusual.

Billy walked up the driveway and let himself in through the back door, which was left unlatched all the time. He went right to his bedroom and slid the backpack off onto his bed, and went to tell his momma he was home.

Velma was in the basement, sewing on a new pair of curtains for the den. She lacked a few inches of having one panel completely hemmed, and she told Billy to go on to the kitchen and get some cookies for himself and his little friend, that she'd be on in just a minute, so Billy headed right back up the stairs.

He set his lunch box down on the kitchen table and got two peanutbutter cookies out of the jar that Velma kept in easy reach. He ate one cookie and two bites of the other one, which he had got out for Barkley like his momma had told him to do, but I guess the Gunnel smarts kicked in because he decided to go look up on the Internet if snakes like peanutbutter cookies. He laid the half-a-cookie beside his lunch box and went off to his room to use the computer Velma and Bill had set up for him, to keep their boy from being left on the wrong side of the technology divide.

Velma sort of lost track of time a little, and she finished up the one panel and started on the other, until she heard the water go on in the shower upstairs and realized Bill was up and getting cleaned up. She put aside her sewing and went up to start breakfast for him. It didn't matter that it was 4:30 in the afternoon. Bill always liked his sausage and egg when he got up.

In the kitchen, Velma put the skillet on, sliced a sausage patty off the roll in the freezer, started a fresh pot of coffee. She set the butter and jelly on the table and picked up Billy's lunch box and set it by the sink, to be washed. She didn't notice it being heavy or anything.

She flipped the sausage, turned down the heat under the skillet, and broke the egg in beside the sausage. She went down the hall to holler at Bill, to tell him that breakfast was nearly ready. He was still in the shower, but he hollered back that he'd be out in a minute. Velma looked in Billy's bedroom as she passed and saw him sitting at his desk, clicking the mouse on the pad with the Jimmy Neutron design on it. She assumed that "Barkley" was on the bed, where she couldn't see him from the doorway.

She went to the kitchen, flipped the egg, turned the stove off, buttered two cut-open biscuits left from hers and the boy's breakfast that morning, and put them in the toaster oven. She went to the sink and ran some hot water, added detergent, and popped open the lid of little Billy's lunch box.

"Bloodcurdling" is how Bill described that scream. Said he hadn't heard anything like it since he helped the vet get that old yellow tom cat out of the Hav-A-Hart trap that had captured a mouse and the cat went in after the mouse and then Jimmy Jarrell's fiest dog that went in after the cat.

Bill come flying out of the bathroom, holding a towel that could barely make the reach around his middle, and slid into the kitchen on Velma's polished linoleum. "What is it?" he shouted. "What's wrong?"

Velma was leaning backwards over a dinette chair,

eyes as big as hen eggs, her face pale and sweaty. She was heaving and gasping. "Snake," she croaked. "Snake, snake, snake, snake, snake, snake."

Bill looked where Velma was looking and saw the last six inches of Barkley pouring off the edge of the counter in the direction of the floor. The back door was not three feet away and I figure Barkley had smelled the great outdoors through the screen, and if Bill or Velma either one had of had their wits about them, they would have opened the door and stood back and let nature take its course, but all the Gunnel smarts in the world does not equal one jot of common sense, and Bill's head was still echoing from that scream, so neither of them did the reasonable thing.

Velma's voice was recovering from its first effort, and now she shouted in a volume that was maybe not Olympics quality but would surely have taken a ribbon at the county hollering contest. "Bill, get that snake out. of. my. HOUSE!"

Always eager to avoid an uproar, Bill went into action as quick as he was able. Still holding the towel shut with one hand, he grabbed a plastic trash can with the other and approached the area where the snake had last been seen, trash can held at the ready, saying gently, "Come here, snake, come on, snake. Come on in here now, let's me and you go out for a little walk."

But Barkley had not waited for an invitation. He had found a medium-sized crack between the side of Velma's cabinet and the wall, and all Bill saw of Barkley was the end of his tail being sucked into the crack, like a dark spaghetti noodle down a pair of pursed lips.

"Well, he's gone into the cabinet," Bill said.

"Bill! Into my cabinet! You get that snake out of there right now!" Velma was pretty excited. "Right now, do you hear? That thing is in there with the potatoes and turnips and I'll have to throw them all out and what if it gets into the dish towels, Bill get him out RIGHT NOW!"

So Bill opened the cabinet doors and looked in, but he couldn't see anything out of the ordinary. It was pretty dark in there. He told Velma he was going to get dressed and get a flashlight, but Velma said no no no, he could not move from in front of that cabinet because what if the snake came out. No, he must stay right there, she'd go get the flashlight.

So Bill got down on his hands and knees and started taking stuff out of the cabinet, carefully, one can of Comet at a time. After a minute he gave up on holding the towel around his middle, and just sort of draped it over his hips, so he could use one hand to lean on and the other hand to lift stuff out.

I guess when he leaned down to see that he wasn't putting his hand into a coil of black snake instead of a pile of potatoes, the towel slipped a little, because he swore that when the next door neighbor's dog, a German Shepherd named Mack, announced himself, there was nothing at all between that dog's wet nose and Bill's privates. It was a close encounter of the worst kind.

Being unused to raising his voice, Bill emitted a kind of gargle and squeal combo, or so Velma said. She was just coming back into the kitchen with the flashlight from the basement plugin where it gets charged up, and she met Mack going out. There was Bill, laying face-up and unconscious in the floor, towel not covering anything but the jelly jar on the table. The black snake was exiting the kitchen by way of the dining room.

Velma called 9-1-1 and Cloatine Blevins, who happened to be the dispatcher on duty, like never to have figured out what was happening at the Bedsaul house. Finally she called the Rescue Squad out for a Code Blue (heart attack). Me and Fred and Jimmy Gleason and Joey Buyers were on call, and we left the building less than five minutes from the time the call came in.

We pulled up in the Bedsaul driveway and me and Fred went in to assess the situation while Joey and Jimmy got the gurney. Velma was in the living room, standing on top of a hassock, and as soon as she said "Bill" and "kitchen," I went on in there to see what was what.

I found Bill laying there, as far out as he could be, but his breathing was easy and his pulse was strong and steady. I found a big punkknot on the back of his head and figured that was the cause of his state, not a heart attack, but I followed the protocols exactly and called for the men to bring the gurney.

I saw the towel on the table, and laid it over Bill.

Velma came back in with the men, which only added to the confusion, because not only were the quarters pretty cramped in there, and we were trying to move the table aside and get Bill on the gurney without dropping him or losing the towel, but she kept talking, loud and fast, all about some snake and how it had gotten into Little Billy's lunch box and then into her cabinets and now it was loose in the house and here was Bill with a heart attack and was he dead or not?

I tried to calm her down. I told her Bill was breathing good and had a steady pulse and might not be having a heart attack at all and did she know what caused that knot on his head?

Velma said she didn't know anything about a knot but if Bill wasn't having a heart attack why wouldn't he wake up and where was that snake?

"What snake are you talking about?" Fred asked, rolling his eyes.

"I told you. I opened the lunch box and it was full of SNAKE, and then it crawled out and went down behind the cabinets and do you think the snake could have hit Bill on the head?"

"Velma, I've never heard of a snake using a weapon," I said. "Now why don't you just step back, out of the way, and we'll take old Bill down to the hospital and get him checked out."

"But where do you think the snake is now?" Velma

asked, just like I'd know. Uniforms affect people that way. You have a uniform on, people think you know all kinds of stuff. "Do you think it's still in the house?"

"Velma, are you sure there was a snake in here?" Fred interrupted. He looked a little sweaty, I thought, but Fred is overweight. "What kind of snake was it?"

"I don't know what kind of snake it was! But it was here, right here in this kitchen, right here on MY COUNTER." Velma was getting teary.

"All right, Velma, why don't you call your brother and get him and Louise to come over. They can drive you to the hospital. Or sit with Little Billy. Where is Little Billy?" I was trying to get Velma's mind off that snake, real or otherwise.

"I told Billy to stay in his bedroom with the door shut," Velma said. Tears were making streaks down her cheeks.

By this time we had Bill loaded. There was no way we could raise the gurney and roll it out of there. I looked around and figured that by lifting the gurney over the top of the table, we could carry him out through the dining room, then out the front door. I told the men the plan and we each took a corner and lifted. We were easing through the dining room door - there was room for the gurney only if we tilted it slightly and kept our hands on the front and back, not on the sides. I was on the right front corner, talking the men through it, when I heard a kind of slipping sound and then, quick, a soft thump.

Then Fred screamed and the gurney with Bill on it was out of my hands and there was a real big crash and clatter and I think Velma screamed, and Jimmy and Joey were hollering and somewhere out back I could hear a dog barking like he was fixing to take off somebody's leg.

Me and Joey seemed to be the only ones alert and able-bodied, or A & A as we say. We checked on Jimmy, who was pretty groggy. He said he thought he'd hit his head on the door frame when Fred dropped his corner of the gurney and the whole thing went down. When he said that we looked around but couldn't see Fred anywhere.

We continued with the triage. We asked Velma to hold Jimmy's hand which mostly shut her up, and then we checked out Bill, who was still dead to the world but seemed no worse than before.

But when we rolled him over on his back, back on the gurney, we began to understand what had happened, for there, underneath Bill and the top rail of the gurney, was a middle-sized black snake, a two-inch section of his middle as flat as a fritter but both ends still wiggling. Bill's arm was caught in the railing, bent at an unlikely angle.

The snake was not in line of view of Velma, which I was glad of. So I wrapped the towel over it right quick and handed it to Jimmy and whispered, "Take this out the back door and get rid of it."

"And see if you can see Fred out there," I called at him as he went out the door.

Later on, when we could get Fred to talk about it, we pieced it all together. The snake had been laying on top of the door between the dining room and the kitchen. When we jiggled the door with the gurney, it lost its grip and slid off, right onto Bill's belly, passing within a foot of Fred's nose on the way down.

Fred has this irrational fear of snakes, and he couldn't help himself. All the EMT training in the world couldn't'uve make him transport a snake, no matter if it was on the belly of a bona fide victim. We don't know where Fred would have got off to, if Mack hadn't cornered him against the privacy fence out back.

The strangest thing was, after we got back from the hospital we wound up going out in the back yard and hunting up that dead snake and bringing it back into the house to show to Velma because we just could not convince her that there wasn't still a snake in her house, crawling around on her clean dish towels and coiling up on her potatoes. So Joey went back out there and got it out of the bush where it had landed when he gave it a heave, and brought it in, and while he was convincing Velma that it was the same snake and was really, truly dead, Little Billy came out from his bedroom and before anybody could prevent him, looked at the dead thing and began such a caterwauling that made even his momma's sound small.

It took a while, but eventually Velma got the whole story from Little Billy.

Despite the knot on his head, which he got when he shot over backwards when the dog nosed his privates, Bill did not have a concussion, but he did get a broken arm from being dumped off the gurney. We all feel pretty bad about that, particularly Fred.

He didn't have a heart attack, either. It was a pure and simple faint.

It was Jimmy who got a concussion, and he never did even lose consciousness or get much of a knot. That's the way it goes, sometimes.

The final tally was, one loss of consciousness and broken arm; one concussion; one dead snake; one dog banned from his neighbor's house; one woman whose family doctor put her on valium for six weeks with a re-fillable prescription; one little boy who might have been heart-broken over the death of the class pet but who was not allowed to have a pet snake of his own, ever; and one bill for a professional extermination and disinfecting of the entire Bedsaul house.

You know how insurance is, and you know how the Bedsauls hate to make a fuss about anything. I'll bet Bill would just about rather have paid for everything out of his own pocket, than try to make the insurance understand and pay up.

Leola's Story

Leola's consciousness hovers some three feet above her body, which is tethered to the hospital bed the family moved into the middle room of the old farmhouse more than two years ago. Leola will be 102 years old in two weeks, if the machines and medicines keep doing their duty and nobody notices that her spirit has - mostly - taken leave of its shell.

Someone is always in attendance, and sometimes more people come into the room with its complicated set-up of pads, blankets, tubes and soft-toned machines. When visitors come, they spend a few minutes lined up at the bedside, like congregants at a communion rail, eager to take whatever it is they imagine she could give them. They speak, some loudly demanding that Leola hear their requests - Honey, can you hear me? Do you know who this is? It's Ruth, come to see you. - and some whispering, as people do in the presence of the dead: Oh, look at her, poor old thing. Don't she look good, though, for the shape she's in?

Very little of it matters to Leola. She is seldom in the stuffy room with its old furniture pushed together to accommodate the metal-railed bed. Mostly she roams the

69

dark, gentle fog that is her world now. In its warm and supportive ether Leola rests, content, washed by gentle currents and upheld by tender waves of darkness that soothe her and give her peace, finally, from everything. Occasionally the darkness debouches Leola gently onto the shore of some memory, washing her in with the smoothest of tides to repose, one tiny bit of debris among the blackened twigs and husks left by other wavelets, and her past plays itself in scenes in front of her while she rests.

Rarely – more and more rarely, it seems – the present breaks into the gentle darkness of Leola's existence. It is so hard to bring herself back to that place; it takes such energy to push air into the lungs, force the throat to constrict, twist the tongue into words. She's nearly forgotten how to do it, and she has little desire to locate and use the strength necessary to accomplish it. Only certain stimuli can rouse her.

"N-o-o-o-o-o-o-o-o-o."

"Did you hear that? What did she say?"

"She doesn't like that, does she?"

"Leola, can you hear me? You don't like that old needle, do you? Do you think she knows we're here?"

"I don't know." This voice, though quavery, carries the careful diction and enunciation of Miss Burwell's elocution classes. The familiar voice sinks to a sigh. "I doubt it."

Miss Burwell, a spinster who stood tall and erect as a fencepost, had taught at Green Pines School long enough to be on her third generation of students: spelling to the second and third-graders, Virginia state history to the fourth and fifth, English or Language Arts to the others. But the most important, to her, was the Elocution Class reserved for the tenth- and eleventh-grade girls. She saw this as her last chance to save them from having the rest of their lives short-changed by their circumstances. They could be ladies, assets to their families and their communities, able to hold their heads up in any social setting, if they would accept the polish and grace Miss Burwell poured over them day after day: speak well, do not settle for the rustic accent of your neighbors; keep topics of discussion ladylike and genteel; sit up, stand tall, do not laugh in a vulgar manner; be gracious and kind but do not give in to the common or base. Above all, speak correctly and with the accents of the educated.

Leola laughed and made jokes about Miss Burwell, even in her classroom. But Lucille, her six-years-younger sister, fell into it like a cat getting into the cream. She grabbed the clipped, careful speech of Miss Burwell at age 16, and never let go of it. Even now, even after all these years and all they knew about each other, sitting here in Leola's sickroom, she talked like the crusading – *turned funny, if you know what I mean, always patting the girls' hands and rubbing their backs* – Yankee school marm that Miss Burwell had been.

"Here, hand her her baby. That always calms her down."

"Her baby? What do you mean?"

"This is her baby. Here, honey, you hold the baby. That's it, nurse the baby."

"Lucille?"

"They got her that doll for her birthday last year. She took right to it; it does seem to calm her."

"I've never known her to have a doll before, not even when we were little."

After finishing at Green Pines, Leola took the secretarial course in nearby Abingdon and went right to work. It was fun. Leola enjoyed having her own money, even though Daddy made her start paying rent for her room at home (since she wasn't doing any chores around the place, he'd said), and she spent it as fast as she earned it: lunches at the counter in the dime store; movies in Bristol; fancy dresses and shoes. She went out with men, too, going with them in the cars that had become common after the war. She even learned to drive, and eventually bought a second-hand car of her own. Her father disapproved.

"Leola, how can you afford this?"

"Daddy, there's such a thing as buying on credit, you know. Auto dealerships are dying to put their customers into good cars!"

"Credit? Buying on credit will get you in trouble. What if this dealer called in your note? Could you pay it off?"

"He's not going to do that, Daddy. It's me and about a million other people. Roscoe Russell could not possibly need all the money everyone owes him for new and used Fords."

Her father, short and stocky, dressed in khaki work pants and a dark wool jacket, turned away. "Leola," he said, with the tone of someone making a beginning.

"Daddy," she interrupted him - to his relief, she thought -- "don't wait up for me tonight. After work, some of the girls and me are going to Bristol to see that new store they've opened up on State Street."

"Leola," he continued doggedly, "your mother and I are worried about you."

"I know."

"Well, thanks for that!"

"But you don't know the ways of the world."

"Now, what ways would you be talking about, exactly?" she teased him. She was usually able to humor him out of a lecture, but this time he remained serious.

"You know what ways." Her father looked straight into Leola's eyes. "Man ways."

She raised her eyebrows and kept her gaze steady, but her cheeks flushed. "I can take care of myself," she said.

"Now listen, you don't know half what you think you do."

"Oh no?" She was really mad, now, more angry than the situation should have meant. But there was something about her father's interference and his... lack of respect that lit a fire in Leola's belly that day. "Then why didn't you tell me to be careful when I was twelve years old, Daddy? How about when I was ten? Eight? All those times Uncle John came to visit?"

His face showed his shock, and something else. Not surprise, but a dreaded confirmation. "Uncle John?"

Leola noticed that foreknowledge. "Uncle John. He's a man, ain't he? Why weren't you worried about me back then? Why didn't you take care of me then?"

Her father turned away from her. He stood, back ramrod straight, hand clenching the handle of the pitchfork he'd been using to lift the dried cow flops from the dirt barn floor, loading them onto a wheelbarrow that waited nearby. The manure would go, Leola knew, into the fields or onto the big vegetable garden beside the house. Nothing was wasted on this farm, nor anything left in an unsightly position, where the neighbors might see it and take it as a sign of laziness. Her father ran the farm with determination and pure, physical strength and if he required that everyone on the place give 16 hours a day to it, he gave no less of himself. She watched his hand on the sweat-smoothed wooden handle, saw it shaking. She saw his shoulders, strong enough to guide the team of Percherons and the plow into straight furrows through rocky new ground, sink.

Leola, floating in her sweet ether, remembers that during that scene, on that warm spring day when she was 20, her young guts had twisted and her breath had come short. (How strong she had been then, and how pretty, too, in the way that the old, rounded mountains are pretty, or those matched horses her father had had: powerful in the hips and shoulders, richly colored and natural.) She'd been angry and resentful and a terrible, terrible pain, a boil long since fleshed over and hidden but still encysted and infected, had throbbed and threatened to burst. But now she feels nothing, barely even any interest in the events or people she's watching.

"Daughter, are you saying-" Her father's voice was dim, sounding still contained in his chest, not released into the open air.

"I'm not saying anything."

"He is your mother's uncle, her favorite, and-"

"I know, and he was the tom cat's kitten! Remembe- how everyone used to say that, that John Hilton was the tom cat's kitten?" Leola stopped, took a breath, and made her voice sound calm and confident. "Daddy, everything is fine."

She wanted to add, everything is fine *now*, Daddy. It's fine because I made myself be strong, and because I kept it all quiet and kept peace in the family. And now because I am strong, I can work and make money and get off this farm and enjoy life, like I thought I would never be able to do. But all she said was, "I will be careful and I will be safe. I'll bring you something from that new store. They say it's a sight to be- hold."

The two stood for a long moment, but the man did not turn to face his daughter. Finally she stepped closer, then hesitated, wanting to touch him but prevented by the natural reticence of the man. She could smell him, old wool and boot grease and tobacco, and unconsciously she leaned nearer. He tilted his face toward the floor, and the old felt hat riding on the rim of tanned skin on his forehead lifted slightly, reveal- ing a strip of soft, pink flesh.

"Your sister," he said softly. "Did John..."

Leola held her breath for one moment, and blinked hard. Then she straightened and turned, saying, "Lucille's fine, Daddy. I always took care of Lucille."

He put his other hand on the pitchfork handle, slid the prongs under a pile of manure, and lifted it to the wheelbar- row. "I don't need anything from that store," he said.

For a moment, Leola feels the doll in her arms. Its body is made of pink cloth, stuffed with something that is soft yet resistant. It weighs and cuddles like a real baby, but its feet and hands are hard and cold, and it smells like plastic and antiseptic, from the disposable wipes they use to keep it safe for her. She is sometimes puzzled by this counterfeit and sometimes willing to pretend along with them, but she is never fooled. She knows what a real baby feels like.

"She never had any children?"

"No. She never married. But Aunt Sarah used to say that Leola was in love with Lucille's husband."

"With Rick? Really?"

"T-a-a-a-a-a-k-e i-i-i-t." From a distance, Leola hears the long, slurred syllables. It is several seconds before she realizes the sound is her own voice, and for a moment she feels the texture of the satin pillowcase under her cheek as she shakes her head.

Oh, he was a good-looking man. When Lucille brought him home, he was in uniform. The Air Force.

Lucille went to college. No secretarial course for her, and no rent to pay while she attended Virginia Intermount College for Women. Of course, in those days there were only two or three options for young women: marriage and homemaking (the most desirable), office work (not quite respectable), or teaching (the storehouse of widows and spinsters). Lucille, tiny as a bird and drab as a sparrow, was too small to be much help on the farm. She seemed too shy and frail for secretarial work and too much of a homebody (to put it kindly. It would have been more honest to have named her homely.) to attract a husband. She had maintained an A average in school, so her application was sent and the big steamer trunk was packed. Off she went and her future seemed secure if not bright. She would become a fine teacher, dressing always in navy and brown, wearing always sensible shoes with low heels, accessorizing each day's dress with half-glasses on a cord around her neck, stockpiling little blue bottles of Evening in Paris cologne with the lace-edged handkerchiefs her students would give her at Christmas.

Leola, concerned about how her little sister was getting along in the real world, drove to the college and pulled up outside the dorm to which they addressed all the letters and packages the family sent. To her surprise, the "dorm" turned out to be an elegant old house, with white columns on the front porch and lace curtains at all the windows. As she was sitting in the car, looking at the imposing structure, a small group of girls swooped out of the front door and down the sidewalk towards the street. They were dressed in pastel sweater sets and dark skirts, with books clutched to their chests or resting on their hips. Their voices were like birds' as they gabbled and twittered among themselves, and in the middle of the flock, to Leola's surprise, walked Lucille.

Leola started to open the door and speak to Lucille. Hey, little sister, where ya' going? Something casual, something fun. She wasn't checking up on her, she was only there to make sure Lucille wasn't suffering, wasn't homesick and lonely. She certainly wasn't there because she missed Lucille, or anything like that.

But it was clear that Lucille was not homesick or lonely, there in the midst of the young girls who looked so much like her: bright, eager, care-free. Leola turned her head, pretended to look into her purse on the seat beside her. She had traded cars just two weeks earlier, and Lucille wouldn't recognize this one. She burrowed through the purse, pushed something onto the floor, bent low to retrieve it from under the seat. When Leola straightened, the gaggle of girls was well past the car, heading for the comer and the crosswalk to the college library. After they'd crossed the street, Leola started her car and drove up Middle Street, toward home.

Leola withdraws from the body in the hospital bed and

lifts into the darkness. She feels she is being rocked, a baby resting on her mother's bosom or a child pushed gently in a swing. Softly, gently, to and fro, she sinks to another level of the deep: sleep, and dreams.

Richard Stewart Macintyre was a handsome man, and nobody could figure out how little old maid school teacher Lucille Anderson ever met him, much less reeled him in to the point of bringing him home to meet her father. She had been teaching for nearly eight years, by then. There was a year at that terrible little school in the mountains, where two teachers taught grades one through eleven, and there were no "facilities."

"There was a toilet behind a row of hawthorn trees," Lucille reported with a shudder, "and water in a bucket in the back of the room."

She had boarded with a nice family near the school building, but one year there had been more than enough, and she came home and landed a position at Green Pines, where her mentor Miss Burwell still held her position. People in the community nodded and spoke elliptically of Lucille being *well-suited* for the work and the place.

Lucille had not learned to drive, so Daddy bought a two-year old Ford (Leola knew beyond doubt and without asking that he had paid cash for it.) and took her in each morning, after finishing the morning chores, and went back to pick her up each afternoon.

Leola had moved to her own place in Abingdon, had moved to the position of assistant to the boss's assistant, and had moved into a higher circle of society. She and her friends had survived the worst of the Depression years by living cheap and sharing whatever good times came their way, and by 1942, things were gearing up. There was an excitement in the air, a sense of things getting under way, that suited Leola. She ignored her family's pointed questions about her marital status, her lack of children, her casual and frequent absences from church, and everything else that it seemed to them a decent woman of certain years should be and do but that Leola wasn't being and doing, and lived pretty much as she pleased.

She did go home every Sunday, if not in time for church then for a nice afternoon visit. On the third Sunday in April, when her father's apple trees were beginning to bloom and redbud trees were painting purple splotches on the mountainsides, there was another guest at the big dining room table. Leola, who had fought long and hard to earn the status of "guest" and not simply that of a daughter who was living in town during the week but was still part of the household at the old homeplace, was surprised to find a young man in uniform between herself and Lucille. She was also amused to see the flush of color across Lucille's cheeks, and hear her voice raised in animated conversation. Lucille even made a joke or two, poking gentle fun at herself for her "country ways" and at their home for its rural nature. Leola thought Miss Burwell's effect was more than usually evident in her little sister's voice, that afternoon.

"Of course, Momma chooses to continue to prepare our meals on the woodburning stove," she heard Lucille say brightly. "Daddy has offered to replace it with an electric appliance, but she wants to continue in the manner to which she is accustomed."

Leola laughed, and started to point out that her father hadn't turned loose enough cash money to buy an electric stove because he'd bought the Ford to deliver and fetch Lucille from school, but she happened to look at her mother's face at that moment, and she fell silent. Then she asked, as she forked up a bite of mashed potatoes and gravy, "Tell us about your home, Mr. McIntyre. Did you grow up on a farm?"

"No, my father worked in the steel mills in Bethlehem, Pennsylvania. As an accountant. "

"Bethlehem a pretty big town?" Leola's father asked. Leola's eyebrows raised with the understanding that her father was already calculating how far away his youngest

78

daughter would be and in what conditions she would be living, if she married this man.

"Population's about eight thousand. Steel's the biggest industry, with the railroads that serve it. I don't plan to go into it, myself."

Leola decided she liked the timbre of Rick McIntyre's voice, deep and confident, and she was aware of the warmth of his shoulder, inches from her own. She tried to be subtle as she laid her fork on her plate, positioned her elbow casually on the edge of the table, and leaned slightly forward, so she could see Lucille's face, on the other side of Mr. McIntyre's chest. She'd assumed, coming in late as she had and missing all the pre-dinner discussion, that the stranger was here on some farm business with her father. Now she understood that the business had nothing to do with the farm, and was all about Lucille. She was surprised, delighted, and amused. The little bird has caught herself a real rooster, Leola thought. How had she done it, and where on earth had they met?

Never one to hesitate, Leola moved her head back just enough to look straight into Mr. McIntyre's face without lifting her chin from her hand, and asked. "How did you meet my little sister?"

From the corner of her eye, Leola saw her mother lift her head; just beyond the dark uniform jacket, Lucille's face flushed deeply pink and then went white.

Mr. McIntyre seemed oblivious. "There was a lecture," he said, "sponsored by the First Methodist Church in Bristol. I was visiting my sister, who teaches at VI. I believe she and Lucille were friends while they were both students there."

"That's right. We were - are - sorority sisters," Lucille interrupted. Leola noticed again, how her dark little eyes glittered.

"Elizabeth - my sister - had arranged to meet Lucille at the lecture, so of course I told her not to change her plans. I just tagged along."

"Uh-huh." Leola couldn't help teasing a little. "And

dare I ask what the subject of this lecture was?"

"The Japanese campaign to establish control of Pacific shipping routes."

"Well, that sounds fascinating." Leola leaned back in her seat, controlling her urge to laugh.

"Yes," Mr. McIntyre continued. "You know, the whole world is watching the war in Europe, but nobody's paying attention to the Japanese. I believe Tojo is as much a menace as Hitler. The Japs-"

"Would you like more bread?" Lucille held the plate of biscuits in front of Mr. McIntyre. Leola half expected this interesting man to snap at Lucille for interrupting, but after a second's pause, he smiled at Lucille and took the plate from her hands.

"No, thank you. Would you?" He turned to offer the food to Leola.

"Well, I believe I will. I just love Momma's biscuits. That old woodstove bakes 'em just right," she said, picking one up. "I like a biscuit that's brown and crisp on the outside and moist and tender on the inside. Don't you, Mr. McIntyre?"

"I haven't much experience with biscuits," he answered. He kept his eyes on his food.

"What? You haven't had biscuits?" Leola was aware of her mother staring, but she kept her own eyes on Mr. McIntyre's profile. "Don't your people eat bread, Mr. McIntyre? It's the staff of life. you know. Around here, we have hot bread two or three times a day. Biscuits, cornbread, loaf bread, griddle cakes. Why, I don't know how we'd get ourselves out of bed in the mornings, if we didn't have Momma's good hot biscuits coming out of the oven to meet us halfway."

"At home, we usually buy bread from the bakery."

"Oh, really? No one in your momma's house bakes, Mr. McIntyre? Why, that's a new idea for folks around here! It sounds a little scandalous; I don't know what a woman would do with all that extra time on her hands. Might lead to mischief." Leola couldn't seem to stop herself. He was so tightly packaged, there beside her in the dark blue uniform with the tie all tucked in and his shoes all shined.

"I think it sounds wonderful."

Leola was astonished that Lucille had cut into the banter.

"In the modern world, some women may even continue to work outside the home, after marriage."

Imagine that, Lucille trying hard to make real conversation with a man, Leola thought.

After a few seconds' pause, Leola leaned forward so she could see her younger sister's face. "Is that so?" she asked, and shot a glance at Mr. McIntyre, who examined his plate as if it were an historical document.

The scene dissolves, and Leola drifts, drifts. Other memories rise from the depths to bump against her mind: more men in uniforms, boys from the neighborhood and men who rode the trains to and from places where they prepared for battle; radio news and newsreels between double features at the theater; hustle and hurry and always the farm and its demands. Faces light and fade before her, and some Leola recalls with pale shades of emotions, while others signify nothing. Throughout her travel in the sweet darkness, Rick McIntyre's image rises again and again. From the time Lucille brought him home to try her mother's good bread and face her father's restrained examination, Rick was part of Leola's life.

"Can we help you turn her over? Lord, ain't she heavy?"

"Look, been laying here two year, and not a bit of a bedsore. They sure do take good care of her."

"And ain't she lucky to be able to be kept at home. It must cost a fortune."

"Yes, I guess this farm is going a piece at a time, to

pay for it all."

"Abra'm Anderson would roll over in his grave."

"Yes, Lord. He would."

A few minutes later Rick followed her to the barn, going first to the shed and looking at the plow. Not that he'd even know how to hitch the horses to it, Leola thought. She watched him stroll casually across the barnlot, avoiding the freshest of the cowpiles without seeming to pay too much attention to them. No, he'd never do such a vulgar thing as openly acknowledge the existence of cow shit, she thought. She went through the feed room and up the stairs to the big loft where the stalks of tobacco hung from two levels of rafters, the long brown leaves like the soft pelts of some musky animal. She breathed deeply to take in the sweet scent of the tobacco. She always liked being here, with its crazy combination of space and confinement - the wide open loft, as big as the entire barn without the dissection of the stalls and rooms on the ground level, and the mobile screens of the tobacco. The big sliding doors were kept adjusted to let air circulate and moisture seep in, to bring the tobacco "to case," when it would be dry enough to not rot yet moist enough to not shatter at a touch. Leola ran her hand gently down a five-foot stalk, noticing the short, tattered leaves near the bottom; the big, light-colored leaves in the middle; and the little, "bright" leaves at the top. By their feel and by their rustle, she knew they were ready to be gathered into the small bundles called "hands" and packed onto flat baskets, then to be shipped to the warehouses in Abingdon.

Leola usually went to the barn loft to be alone, but she was neither surprised nor displeased when she sensed Rick McIntyre close behind her. She'd left the feed room door open. "I always liked working off the tobacco," she said quietly.

"I thought you hated farm work."

"I do, but this is different. It doesn't make you sweat.

It's the fall of the year, when the rest of the farm is shutting down, and sometimes we do it at night, with lanterns in the barn. They make a pretty light, and the women talk in whispers, and the tobacco leaves sigh and swish."

"You make it sound like a poem."

She stepped away, and he stepped closer. "It's one of the few things women are allowed to do without the men being in charge. All the men stay in, all except Daddy. He's here, stripping off the leaves and bringing them to us, sorting them into piles on the wagon bed. But he doesn't speak. It's our work. He just... it's like he's our servant."

"Is that what you like? Men waiting on you?" He stepped closer again, coming up behind her, and now she felt his breath on her hair and smelled his smell, his aftershave and sweat, all around her.

She breathed deeply, taking in the tobacco and him, and closed her eyes. The word *servant* is wrong, she thought. It's something like that but different, it's something almost holy. In her mind, a picture rose of a man in a short tunic who walked carefully to a low altar and positioned a bundle of sweet herbs at the feet of a matronly figure in white. *Acolyte.*

"I've heard worse ideas," she said, making the image dissolve.

He didn't speak, but bent his head so his face was in her hair. He turned his lips against her scalp, followed the curve of her skull to her ear, to the comer of her jaw, to the cheekbone just under her eye.

Soon after that, he shipped out. While he was away Lucille wrote to him twice a week, as steady as the pendulum on a clock, and seemed to grow a little smaller and drier while she waited. He wrote back sporadically; Lucille claimed some of his letters had gone astray. Leola didn't write at all. She kept herself busy, making sandwiches for the boys on the trains, dancing at the USO benefits in town, and working. There was a lot of demand for women to work, in those days; the country needed factory workers and secretaries and all kinds of help for the war effort. It had been exciting, and things had felt wide open and thick with chances for strong and self-sufficient women. Then it was over, and as the men came home, the jobs went back to them.

After Rick had been back in the States for a month, and after he'd spent a few days with his mother in Bethlehem, he'd come calling at the farm. They all assumed he'd come to court Lucille, little wren Lucille who in his absence had gone to work every day and who had aged from 29 - nearly too old, even then nearly an old maid, nearly a spinster, nearly so set in the shape of a schoolteacher that hope had barely held up her face and figure - to 33. Lucille must have felt her light was nearly extinguished, Leola thought. Lucille, the child whom she'd protected and guarded from men, was now a woman desperate to have a husband, and a life.

But then, again, Rick followed Leola into the barn.

Leola stood still, her knees trembling with desire for this man.

He put his hands on her arms, bare in the soft fall weather; moved them to her shoulders, across her chest, cupped her breasts.

"Mr. McIntyre?" she whispered.

"Miss Anderson," he answered.

She allowed the lids of her eyes to slowly close and asked, "Is this a proposal?" He raised his head but did not move his hands. "A proposal?" His voice was even and calm. "What kind of proposal do you mean?"

"You know what kind."

He lowered his hands to her ribs, pulled her firmly against him, wrapped his arms around her body. Against her ear, he whispered, "You know what I need."

Leola breathed deeply, took thought, said, "A lot of people around here have needs. You, me. Lucille."

He raised his head but kept his arms around her.

"Lucille."

She knew, right then. But she let herself pretend for a few more seconds. "Just what are your intentions regarding Miss Lucille Anderson, Mr. McIntyre?"

Her turned her in his embrace, held her against him, rubbed his hands down her back and over her buttocks. He pulled her even more tightly against him. "I intend to marry Miss Lucille Anderson."

She was ready. She could say, without the least hesitation, "And do you intend to make her happy? Do you intend to give her everything she wants?"

"Oh yes," he said, hands still in place, warm and insistent. "I understand everything about Miss Lucille." He nuzzled Leola's neck. "And I understand you," he said.

Oh, no you don't, she thought. No, you don't. But she knew how to control crying, and as she led Rick McIntyre to the corner where the old quilts used to cover the baskets of tobacco were stacked, she pictured an acolyte kneeling before a goddess in a temple lit with lantern light.

"R-i-i-i-i-i-i-i-i-i-kuh. R-i-i-i-i-i-i-i-kuh!"

"What's she saying? What's she saying, Lucille? Can you tell?"

"No, I have no idea. It probably doesn't mean anything."

Above her body, Leola's consciousness waits. There is something else, she knows, something that's keeping her from leaving. And she knows that if she could figure out what that is, she'd grab it, swallow it, breathe it, choke it, whatever it would take to get it done and leave here. She wants so much to be gone.

"How long is Lucille staying? Who came down with her, this time?"

"That's one of her grandsons, that drove her down.

She's going to stay until the end, she says, but he's going back to Pennsylvania tomorrow."

"How many grandchildren does she have?"

"I forget. Let's see, she has two children, Ricky and Linda, and they both had a couple of children... Lord, I don't know, I can't keep up with 'em."

"Ain't it wonderful, how devoted she is to her sister? They were always real close."

"Oh yes, close as can be."

"Poor old Leola. She don't have anybody but Lucille."

In the darkness there is peace and calm but for the memories that now bump and nuzzle, like piglets at the sow. They bump, bump, nudge, seeking life from Leola who wearily lies back in the dark and gives them suck.

There's herself at work in town, well past forty and understanding, at last, her own capabilities - just as the administrator promotes a less qualified "girl." There are new cars and boyfriends and movies and the great carbuncle of pain that Leola refuses to lance, and there is Rick and coupling in the secret dark. There's the day Daddy comes to town to tell her to come home; they need her. Momma can't keep up with it all any more, and the farm work has to be done, and Leola is the only one, she's the unwed daughter, she has to come home and take up the reins.

There was no apology. Daddy stood in the living room of her apartment, his hat in his hand, and wouldn't even sit down. It was as if he expected Leola to pick up her purse and walk out the door with him, as if almost 20 years of living on her own wouldn't have left her with... things, and obligations, and people that she'd have to tell.

"Sit down, Daddy," she said, and watched as his pale eyes swept the room with its big, soft chair and couch, coffee table with magazines and ash trays, and oil heater. She realized with surprise that she'd never seen her father sit in

86

anything but a straight backed, bark-bottomed chair, either at the kitchen or dining room table, or by the wood stove in the kitchen where the family sat in the evenings in winter, or in the same chair carried out to the porch in the summer.

"I have a job," she said.

He didn't even reply. For him, a "job" did not signify; it wasn't real work, the life-sustaining effort that laid a line from earth to hand to table. It wasn't family.

She couldn't bring herself to say, "I have friends. I have a place here." For him, none of that mattered. She was his daughter and obedience was required of her and everything she had done away from that farm had been more or less frivolous ways of marking time - at his generosity - until she came home.

She would have argued against it. She might even have simply ignored his demand and stayed where she was or gone to some other city. It would have meant losing him and all contact with her parents - maybe her whole family - but she might have gone. But there was something else, someone else she had to consider.

Eventually, after fewer minutes than any of her friends would have believed, she nodded. "I need a few days to clear up things here," she said.

He looked a question at her.

"I have to work out a few days' notice, and collect my paycheck. I have to do something with this furniture, see about the lease."

He looked around again. "Do you want me to send a man with a truck?"

She looked around too, seeing it all differently, now. "No. I can probably sell most of it. If you'll come back on Saturday, in the car, we'll get it all in there."

He nodded, and turned to leave. There was no word of thanks, no acknowledgement of anything she'd accomplished or sacrificed.

Maybe that was for the best.

Although it seems that Leola has floated in the sweet, deep darkness for a long time, and she'd thought - in the vague half-dreamed believing that is as much thinking as she does, here - she was held and cradled by tides that went nowhere, she now is sensible of a pulling, of a drawing towards something. If she had had strength, she would have, at first, resisted. Finally, though - and there is a subtle sense of finality - she gives in to it and even turns towards it. Whatever it is to which she is drawing near, it is the last.

The memories flip like the pages of a cartoon book, with characters that appear to move because each panel is drawn slightly differently from the one before it. One sequence shows a woman standing still, tall and strong, then shows her heavier, slower, even more still, then dividing in two; she is diminished. One is of a small figure, bright eyed and apparently weak, that evolves, through the gradual metamorphoses of arms into wings, hands into talons, mouth into beak, into a bird of prey, or harpy. The mother figure squats, melts, becomes motionless, an intake and outlet for simple physical need. One man becomes less and less dimensional and is finally nothing more than a stick figure, going through the motions of hard physical labor; the other does not change at all.

Everything had worked out for the best. The move home had come so obviously because of her family's need, there was never any question of it being an excuse for her disappearance. She was so old, (approaching her 43rd birthday) that most people thought a pregnancy unlikely if not impossible, and with all the carrying on she'd done over the years, surely she knew how to not get caught. And she was so stout and strong, not even the closest members of her family had realized what was happening until the last few weeks. Her father, familiar as he was with the fecundity of livestock, had finally admitted what was before his eyes. He'd resisted knowing until the day she went into labor, and then he'd asked if he should go for the doctor. Leola, leaning against the kitchen table and panting with the contraction, had nodded.

"What do you reckon is the matter with her? She must be in pain. Why is she making that noise?"
"Here, you hold her down and I'll give her a shot. Come on now honey, this will make you feel better. You just hold on."

"Hold on to this strap, Leola. Pull against it. Pull!"
"Doctor, shouldn't I be at the hospital? Shouldn't I-"
"Come on now, Leola. You're not a silly girl, you're a big, strong woman. You got yourself into this mess and now you don't want to be shaming your whole family with it. Just get this baby born and no one needs know anything about it."

Leola panted and grunted and pulled on the strap. Finally, with the feel of an enormous clot slipping out, the baby emerged. The old doctor wrapped the gooey baby in one of Momma's white towels, used one comer to wipe the baby's face and chest, and laid it on a stack of newspaper in the corner.

"Give him to me! Give him to me!" she shrieked, and although he frowned, he returned the infant to Leola, muttering, "Be quiet. It would be better if you never saw or touched it."

Leola held the baby and saw Rick's chin and forehead. She lifted the towel and saw that he was a beautiful baby, with tiny, elegantly defined fingers and toes. He turned his face toward her and uttered a tiny, mewling cry, and her breasts tingled and tightened.

While the doctor packed padding between her legs, Leola unbuttoned the man's work shirt, washed to the softness of suede, that she wore, and lifted her baby to her breast. He blindly nuzzled and searched, then began to nurse, and Leola felt that a great, aching bruise she hadn't even known was there in her chest, around her heart, began to heal. She closed her eyes and sighed, and relaxed against the bed's headboard.

Instead of helping Leola into clean clothes and freshening her bed, the doctor threw a blanket over her and her baby and left the bedroom. Leola did not even notice. Eventually, she got her bed and herself cleaned up. She bathed the baby in warm water poured from the big pitcher into the matching basin, brushing away the last signs of his gestation and christening him in the good spring water of the farm.

Over the next few days, Leola nursed and changed the baby and kept her own needs met - telling her father to open home-canned jars of soup and pork with gravy, to heat on the kitchen stove - and stayed in the upstairs room. She took not one thought of what the others said, did, or thought. The only things in her heart and mind were the baby and, much more distantly, his father.

Leola hadn't expected to see Lucille for weeks yet, and she was startled when she looked up from nursing her son and saw her sister standing in the open doorway. Lucille was dressed handsomely, in an expensive dress and matching sweater, with shoes that, though subtle and dark-colored, were beautiful. A matching bag hung from its strap across her shoulder.

A wave of warmth rose in Leola. Her affection for this sister had been a sweet precursor of the love that now bound her to her son. She might not have been able to love him so well if she had not loved Lucille first. And she thought this woman, perhaps alone of all others, would be able to set aside society's ire and accept this beautiful gift she and the family had been given. Lucille would never know, she prayed, who was the father of this baby, but how could her sister help but love him? The baby was beautiful, perfect.

Lucille crossed the threshold and closed the door softly behind her. She walked slowly to the bedside and looked at Leola's face.

90

Leola fancied she could feel love radiating from her own cheeks and forehead like lamplight. "Lookie what I got," she said.

Lucille didn't look at the baby. "Are you all right?" she asked, almost whispering.

"Yes, I'm fine." Leola was disappointed that Lucille hadn't even looked at the baby, but then... She saw the beautiful dress, held to Lucille's trim waist with a leather belt that matched the shoes and purse. Lucille and Rick had been married three years, and there had been no sign of a pregnancy. Maybe if she touched this beautiful new baby, if Lucille felt the sweet warmth of this tiny body, then whatever knot was tied in her guts would loosen. Maybe then Rick's seed could take hold in her. "Look. Look, Lucy. He's a beautiful little boy."

Leola saw the muscles in Lucille's jaws move and tighten. She saw cords rise to the surface of her neck, just under the skin that was - to Leola's surprise - beginning to thin and look fragile. Lucille tilted her head and looked at the baby in Leola's arms.

He slept, undisturbed by their quiet conversation, his dark eyelashes resting on his fresh cheeks. As Lucille stared, his jaws moved and the tiny pink lips let go of Leola's nipple. Leola, who had been so enraptured by the baby that she was completely unaware of her own body, saw a dark flush suddenly rising in her sister's face. At first puzzled, she soon moved the baby to her other arm and pulled her clothing over her breast. Desperate to make a connection between these two people she loved above all others, she held the baby up, pushing him against Lucille's body. "Here, you hold him while I get up."

Hesitantly, Lucille took the baby into her arms. She stood straight and still, and Leola, watching, thought the magic was starting to happen; the baby was bridging the gap that Lucille had cut around herself. It's the smell of him, Leola thought, the smell of him alone would be enough to melt the heart of an icicle.

Then the flush disappeared from Lucille's face, re-placed by a pallor so intense Leola thought her sister was going to faint. She grabbed the baby and put one arm around Lucille's thin shoulders. "What? What is it? Are you sick?"

Lucille's gaze had not moved from the baby's face.

"Sit down, sister. Put your head down," Leola said, pushing Lucille onto the side of the bed. She turned aside and laid the baby in the big market basket she was using for a cradle, then turned quickly back to Lucille. She sat beside her and put one arm around Lucille's shoulders, pressed her other hand against Lucille's forehead. Lucille wasn't hot with fever, thank God; she was cold and clammy. Leola reached behind them and pulled a small quilt from its place on the foot of the bed. She pulled it around Lucille's shoulders like a shawl. "What happened to you?" she asked.

Lucille didn't answer. She sat staring straight ahead, in the direction of the baby's basket, but Leola thought Lucille didn't actually see it. Leola was beginning to lose the bliss that had enveloped her since her baby's birth. "What is it? What is it?" she demanded, and put both arms around Lu-cille, crushing the smaller woman against her chest.

Lucille pushed out of the embrace, out of the quilt's folds. She stood up and turned, her body visibly shaking. "Whose baby is that?" she asked, her voice a hiss, a tiny drop of spit erupting from the corner of her mouth.

Leola's pulse slowed. "He's my baby," she said.

"And who else's?" Lucille leaned forward, eyes wide and glittering. "Who is the father?"

Leola forced her breath to go in and out slowly, steadily. Her hands did not shake, her eyes did not blink. She looked straight at her sister and answered, "Nobody you know."

Lucille poured her gaze into Leola's as if it were boiling oil, as if secrets and truth would float to the top of it and spill out onto the brown and pink linoleum on the floor, if she looked long enough. Leola did not stir.

Finally, Lucille drew her head back. She drew a deep breath, causing her nostrils to flare. She blinked and when her eyes opened, Leola thought, I don't know who this woman is, or how that body can hold such hate.

Lucille stepped quickly to the door, crossed into the hallway, and slammed the door hard behind her. Leola could hear the sharp click of those fancy heels over the baby's cries.

Later the sharp-clicking heels returned, with her father's heavy, deliberate boot steps. They came into the upstairs bedroom with the little quilt on the bed and the basket in the floor, and they talked and they talked and they talked and when the shoes and the boots finally went away again the basket was gone. The entire room was as empty and barren as the moon.

In the deep darkness above her body, Leola struggles to struggle. She wants to move, to flail her arms and kick her legs. She wants to push, to ram her head into something. She wants to scream, but she cannot make it happen. She is impotent in the flaccid darkness and it is only the memories that have strength and power.

And now they flash across her mind like a slideshow: her baby, now Lucille's (and Rick's, Rick who keeps his eyes away from hers, who never follows her into the barn, who never lets his hand touch hers as they pass the biscuits around the dining room table, meal after meal, year after year, never ever again) as he grows into a boy, then an adolescent. Oh, he looks like Rick, a young Rick, and everyone says so: There's no denying who that child belongs to, they say. Under Lucille's and Rick's tutelage this child is quiet and self-contained, but strong, Leola sees.

The slides shift and change though Leola would like to hold them back. She would have stopped the show on the picture that focuses on that child; but in a flash it's gone.

93

There's a shot of Lucille in a gather-front blouse, her hands covering a big belly. There's surprise but also concern, and voices that express rude conjecture: Isn't she a little old for this? Then there's a second child, a tiny girl dressed in pink dresses over starched petticoats, and shiny black shoes with straps over lace-trimmed socks. She looks like Lucille but brighter, sweeter, less intense.

Another slide falls into place, and Leola sees herself, middle-aged and grim, sitting in a warm nighttime, on the stove wood that is stacked against the garage shed.

She came outside to smoke a cigarette, an activity she refuses to relinquish even though she must hide it from her family. She thinks it is almost the last piece of her from her youth. She's given up almost everything else.

Rick emerges from the yellow-lit kitchen and walks to the rick of cut wood. His eyes have been bathed in the light inside the house; he does not, at first, see her sitting there. He comes close to gather an armload of wood for the old kitchen stove. He feels for the stacked wood, his hands stretching toward her thigh, and he begins to fill his left arm with wood.

Leola doesn't speak, but suddenly he senses her - perhaps he smells her - and he stops, left arm half filled, right hand clutching a stick of split poplar.

She reaches into her apron pocket, pulls a cigarette from the pack and puts it in her mouth, pulls out the box of kitchen matches. Rick hears the sound of the match head sliding across the gritty paper glued to the side of the box, and the quick snap as the tip ignites, followed by the rushing sound of the match tip enflamed. There's a flare of light from the match on Leola's face, deepening her wrinkles and lines for a few seconds, then softening them in the sweet glow of firelight. She shakes the match twice, and the light's extinguished. She holds the matchstick long enough for it to cool slightly, then flicks it into the weeds.

94

"Hello, stranger," she says.

He doesn't speak, but he does linger, lowering the load of wood to rest on the cut stack.

She smokes; he waits.

"He's a good boy, isn't he?" she says, after finishing half the Marlboro.

"I won't talk to you about this," he says, and pulls the wood back against his chest, getting ready to go.

"Does that mean there's something we can talk about?"

He adds another stick to his load, and one more, then turns to go.

"Your girl's a sweet child," she said. She draws deeply on the cigarette, exhales slowly, adds, "Too."

Now he sinks against the wood pile, like he's suddenly too heavy to hold himself up. He doesn't speak, but she waits for him.

"I don't know where she gets it," he says, sounding deeply tired. "There's little enough in me, and her mother. . ."

She smokes until there's almost no cigarette left, but she holds onto it. "Her mother is a tough little bird," she says finally, as she drops the final half-inch of butt onto the ground. It is visible in the darkness, a tiny red drop pulsing with the moving air.

"Her mother," he begins, like the words are climbing their way over a dam, over a big dam, a dam like the Hoover, Leola thinks, miles tall and wide and holding back the mighty Colorado in a lake that has buried all the evidence of ancient history in its path. She'd listened to a radio program put on by the National Geographic company. "You have no idea about her mother."

She wants another cigarette, but she's afraid to distract Rick with the movement of getting one out and lighting it. More than she wants a cigarette, she wants to hear what he will say.

"You think not?" she asks. Quiet, now, she's almost whispering.

He keeps his voice low, but the dam is clearly leaking. Stuff is flowing over, now.

"Why didn't you keep our baby? Why didn't you tell me you were going to have him? Why did you have to give him to her? God, it would've been better if you'd put him on a doorstep somewhere."

Leola feels as if, somewhere inside her, her own little dam is developing a crack.

She hadn't been sure Lucille had ever told Ted where that baby had come from. She'd imagined Lucille wanting to keep her secret, to keep Rick and her from... sharing. She wants to say that she was giving the baby to Rick. Not her. Him. For the sake of the families. But she stays still, wanting to hear all that he will say.

"Do you have any idea how she's held that over me, all these years? How she's used it?"

There are words slipping through the crack in her heart, words that are hot and heavy. "You stayed. You managed to make a baby with her."

He dropped the wood he has held in his arm, turns to her. She senses his clenched fists. "Do you want to know how that happened? She timed it. She counted days on a calendar and she put on a silky nightgown with a blue bow tied under her tits, and then she laid down on the bed. 'All right,' she said. All right, like giving me permission. Or orders. And I went to her and I did it, but it was like working on a mannequin. I tried to kiss her, and her teeth were clenched. And the night after that, it was the same, only, only you know what? She had a different nightgown. And the next night but one? A new nightgown, same routine. It took three months. Three nights each month, all timed out and marked on her calendar. By the third month, I was so sick of it, I couldn't... I couldn't do it any more."

Near their feet, the last bit of cigarette winks out. Leola feels words spilling over inside her, and plucks out a few almost at random. "Where'd she get three pretty nightgowns?"

96

In the dark, she feels that he turns his face toward her. He stares, then laughs. It is weird that he laughs like a banshee but retains control enough to keep it quiet. Years of training, she thinks.

"You want to know where she got the nightgowns?" he demands, laughs, wipes his face with his hands. "From some old teacher she knows, some woman who was her teacher when she was still in high school. It's just like her, isn't it? To keep in touch with some old maid school teacher who was probably some kind of role model for her."

"Miss Burwell?" Leola asks, astonished.

"Yeah, Miss Burwell. They write little notes back and forth. Miss Burwell sends presents, perfume, handkerchiefs. Every year, a nightgown. I used to think it was silly, some old woman sending Lucille a nightgown every year for Valentine's Day. I hate them now. I couldn't take even seeing those gowns again, but she never wears them. I guess she got what she wanted out of them."

Leola feels sick. She fumbles in the apron pocket for a cigarette, lights it, draws the smoke deep into her lungs. It feels clean to her, cleaner than the air around her and Ted.

At the house, the back porch light comes on. They both look at it, waiting, maybe, for someone to come out. No one does.

Leola feels ash fall across her knuckles on its way to the earth. "You'd better get back in there."

He hesitates, gathers up the wood he was sent to get, goes back to the house, moving slowly from the soft darkness towards the bright electric light.

One hundred and two years old, floating three feet above her tired old body, Leola remembers. She pushes back into the shell, almost wincing at the feeling of the bed and the sheets, the tubes and the aches. She uses strength she hasn't remembered she had to roll the head, lift the chest, raise the hand. She urges the tongue to move, to moisten the

97

lips, to swallow, to curl like a wave.

"Lucy," she says, quite clearly for someone in such a condition.

"Did you hear that? Lucille, she's asking for you. Did you hear how plain that was? She said your name, plain as day."

"Leola?" Quavery voice, Miss Burwell's vowels and consonants.

"Lucille, can you-u-u hear-r-r-r-r- me?" Slow, working slowly through this failing body, she speaks.

"Yes, I can hear you."

"Who-o-o-o's-s-s here? Who-o-o-o's with us-s-s-s?"

"It's me, Cousin Leola, it's Mary, and Susie Lee. We're here, too."

Good, she thinks. Family is here, to share the news. There are witnesses. "Lucille?"

"I'm right here."

She feels something dry and cool, touching her body's hand. "L-u-u-u-u-u-c-e-e-e-e." She feels the hush, the leaning in to hear. She puts as much effort as she has left into inflating the lungs, then moving the mouth and throat. Important to get it out clear. "Rick always loved me best."

There is no response from the side of the bed where Lucille is standing. From the other side, where the children of her cousins are standing, there are small gasps, a giggle, a whispered "What does she mean?"

Almost no one hears Leola's last words. The witnesses, the members of the family who happened to come to the old farmhouse where Uncle A'bram and Aunt Sarah had lived, where one of their surviving children has lived these last three years as a spirit floating in memories and where the other has kept bright-eyed watch over every sound uttered by the spirit sister, were engaged in discussing the sudden revival of Cousin Leola. Only Lucille, vigilant to the last but no longer in control, hears her sister say with her last breath, "You old fag."

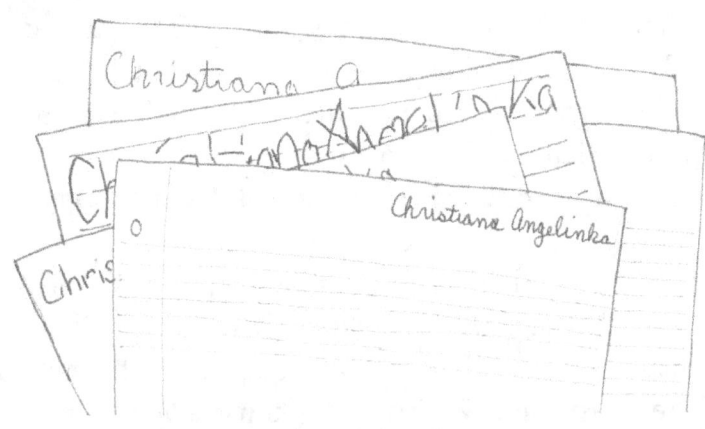

Christiana Angelinka

Christiana Angelinka Rhymeholt came to understand at a very young age that she was different. To begin with, her hair was like no one else's she'd ever seen: the color of coal, it was and always had been three inches long, and curly. Her grandmother, in a fit of familial reminiscence, had once said that her father's hair had been exactly the same. Since he had exited this world from the seat of a Honda Shadow 750 motorcycle two days after Christiana's birth, she had no way to personally verify this information. But it was true that the dark mop curling above her palest blue eyes, tended to disconcert.

Then there was her name. Vaguely Germanic, distinctly lengthy, Christiana Angelinka might have struggled against it; but soon she took it as representative of her very soul and used it as both a talisman and a standard. She had never taken up a nickname, had never, by the simple expedient of not responding to any other salutation, been identified as a Chris, Christy, or Tina; would not pretend to be an Angie, Angel or even, as one too-cheerful kindergarten assistant had suggested, an "Inkie." Near the beginning of second grade, her teacher, a towering, sinuous old dragon permeated with cigarette smoke and 38 years of teaching seven-year-olds to sit still, had instructed the class to write their "full, legal names" on the top lines of paper she handed out. Christiana had sat quietly, hands in lap, after printing her first and last names. They were beautifully done, all a's rounded and horizontals firm and sure, without an erasure or a wobbly perpendicular. The two names quite filled the line; 19 letters and one space were more than all the little Megans, Dakotas and Ambers would ever have to organize.

Nevertheless, when Miss Buchanon stopped to check Christiana's work, the child felt a sharp sting on top of her head and heard a corresponding snap, loud in the strained silence of the classroom. "Why didn't you write your whole name?" Miss Buchanon hissed.

"I don't know how to spell 'Angelinka,'" Christiana answered. She could as easily have said that the name was too long for the space, or just have kept her normal silence, but already, at the age of seven, excuses and pointing out the obvious were not Christiana's style, so she'd answered honestly.

"My god," Miss Buchanon muttered sotto voce, and then Christiana watched while the long-fingered hand with enameled nails laid a bent and broken (explaining the blow to her cranium) pencil on Christiana's desk, picked up Christiana's own pencil, and quickly but accurately drew "A n g e l i n k a" above "C h r i s t i a n a R h y m e h o l t." Christiana had watched, fascinated, and had known she would never, ever again ask about or explain to anyone her long and odd name. The sense of power overcame the humiliation of having a pencil broken over her skull in front of 22 wide-eyed peers, and from that day forward she was and was only, "Christiana Angelinka."

By age 15, Christiana Angelinka had a reputation for being weird, and she understood that the teenagers who shared her high school classes didn't know the half of it. Somehow, word of the little burn marks around the bicep of her left arm had gotten out, but there was more than one - more than 20, actually! – students with little scabs and

102

scars at BHS who had regular weekly sessions with the guidance counselor. Her penchant for black clothing and lipstick didn't really make her unique, since the widespread and televised popularity of the British singer/drug abuser Amy Winehouse had made goth accessorizing not only accepted but also widely emulated. Even her consistently good grades didn't set Christiana as far apart ("from the madd - en - ing crowd" as she thought it with disdain) as it might have. She was only a good student, not one of the real status-seekers, not one of the Top Twenty: climbing into that group would have meant sublimating her individuality to become a teacher's-ass-kisser, theoretically at least, if not in fact.

No, Christiana Angelinka knew that what was unique about herself was her indifference. Most of what seemed to excite and interest the people around her left Christiana cold. Boys and dating were of no interest. She went to a movie with David Finnley because he asked and she couldn't think of a reason not to. Afterwards, she'd turned her face away from his kisses but had allowed his hands to move from her breasts to her underwear and then had lain without protest while he took her virginity, waiting to see if this thing, this event around which so much of her classmates' talk revolved (boys' jokes, girls' whispers, lists of who did and who did not, speculation and repeated information) would engage her body or mind. It did not.

This seemed to drive David crazy. When Christiana turned down his request for a second date, he'd first begged and sworn his love for her, and then, after three rejections, he'd told all the boys in his weight-lifting class that Christiana had "put out" for him and probably would for anybody, now that he'd gotten her addicted to sex. For a while, Christiana had gotten calls from boys who were sniggery or shy, grossly blunt or confusingly obtuse, but she'd answered them all with the same cool indifference as she had David, and eventually they'd stopped.

It was Christiana's remoteness that cooled their heat.

They could have taken in stride an angry retort. They half-expected tears and head-hanging at school; they would have been equally frightened and excited by any form of acquiescence. But her calm, polite turn-downs and her progress through school without any demonstrable evidence that she even understood the situation, was baffling. It counteracted their interest, no matter how fervid, and protected her isolation in a way that at first surprised and then confirmed her vision of herself. She was the ice queen, the otherworldly, the different.

When the senior class trip to Dennison's was announced, Christiana ignored it as she had as much of the other graduation traditions as she could. She had passed on the opportunity to buy a class ring, had declined to order a T-shirt with all her classmates' signatures printed on it (even though her own was easily discernible in the design, due to its length and her neat, legible cursive writing), had ordered not one announcement or little white card with her name imprinted upon it. She would have skipped the graduation ceremony all together if it were not absolutely required in order for her to receive her diploma.

When the sign-up sheets for the Dennison's trip were posted on the cafeteria doors, she walked by them without once stopping to see who was riding on which bus. None of her classmates of thirteen years expected her to. It was the exchange student, Irene, who, while being instructed in the fine art of choosing trip companions of agreeable social status and fun factor (and of course the right ratio of males to females), turned, saw Christiana, and called out, "Christiana Angelinka, which bus are you going to ride to the amusement park?"

Christiana Angelinka stopped, caught more by Irene's beautiful pronunciation of her name than by what she'd said. This girl had insisted that her own name be proniounded the way it had been in her home country: Ee-RAY-nay. From Irene's mouth, in Irene's thick accent, "Christiana

Angelinka" flowed like the Rhine. It sounded beautiful and normal, and in the momentary belief that she was both those things, Christiana Angelinka walked to the doors, smiled at Irene, and looked at the lists.

"Here, I'll put you on the same bus as me. Okay?" Irene asked, and again, the words poured like liquid, bemusing Christiana so that she smiled more. She saw her long, full, legal name going on the list from the tip of the pen held in Irene's hand. Then the bell rang and everyone hurried to class, and Christiana was startled to realize she was going on the class trip to Dennison's Destination, the biggest amusement park east of the Mississippi, featuring eleven roller coasters, a water park, and five food courts.

That morning, Christiana Angelinka got off the bus that had picked her up at the end of her grandmother's driveway, went inside the school just long enough to put her bookbag in her locker, and got on another bus. During the two-hour drive to Dennison's she listened to music on her iPod and dozed, distantly aware that around her, kids were chatting, laughing, trading seats. Girls were adjusting their makeup and talking loudly for the boys' attraction. They were taking pictures of each other with cell phones, and texting each other and students in the other busses. Mrs. Blevins, Christiana's English teacher, sat in Christiana's seat for a while and tried to make conversation, but after futile attempts to engage Christiana with "Have you settled your plans for after graduation?" and "Have you got a job lined up for this summer?" (Answers to both questions: "No."), she'd moved to the front seat and talked to the bus driver.

It was Student Day at Dennison's, and by the time they got there, the huge parking lots were nearly filled with school buses. The chaperones handed out tickets as students clumped wearily off the buses, intoning, "Stick with a buddy," and "Remember where we're parked and be back here at three o'clock sharp."

Christiana wandered the twisting, connected walkways and watched other students, teenagers and middle-schoolers, racing from ride to ride. Many of the younger students were dressed in matching T-shirts, and they darted about in groups like bright tropical fish, schooling up for protection against larger, predatory fish. At the most popular rides, they had to stand in line for up to an hour, and the shrieks from the girls on the roller coasters bled into the shouts of the kids waiting in line, making a thick blanket of noise that spread out over the sounds of the rushing roller coasters and the tinkling, twinkling carnival games.

Christiana felt like she was in a huge zoo, surrounded by the exhibits of exotic creatures, stifled by their shrieks and cries.

Eventually, she made her way to a less-populated side of the park, where the noise was somewhat subdued and the crowds thinned. Here was the auditorium, painted pink, where, later in the season, country-music wanna-bes would sing and smarm their way through three shows a day, with a puppeteer or magician for the kiddies. Behind the auditorium was an old roller coaster, a huge rattling affair that lacked the frenetic fury and visual horror of the newer ones, so although the rides lasted three times as long as the Bolt! or the Verti-Howler, the wait to get on was much shorter. Off to one side was the pavilion that covered the dodge-'em cars. Behind that was a small go-cart track, banked in its turns and watered regularly to keep the red clay surface packed and firm. Beyond that, the noise dropped to the murmur of ocean surf and the asphalt shrank to a simple, wide path in a neatly mowed lawn, and Christiana kept walking.

She became aware that high overhead a gray arch, that had been near the gravel lot where their bus parked, cut through the hazy summer sky. She'd noted the arch as a landmark to guide her back to the bus, and had assumed it was part of some construction project. Perhaps they were building a new, even higher-rise roller coaster, and the arch would support materials being lifted into position. She used it now as a beacon, with the idea of returning to the bus early forming in her feet as much as in her mind.

But the closer she got to the arch, the more it drew her. She felt compelled to look up at its apex, so far away it seemed pale and insubstantial. Its base was hidden by several small buildings that huddled beside it, but she realized it was constructed of metal and that the two legs of the arch actually split into two shafts each, so it was anchored on four feet sunk into concrete. Then Christiana saw that there was a second, smaller construction behind the arch. This was also a slim metal jut into the air, but instead of an arch, it was a tall rectangle – or the outline of one – with one end buried in the earth.

Christiana walked slowly, her feet feeling their own way towards the arch as her eyes were concerned solely with seeing it, measuring it, guessing its texture and strength and her whole body was yearning, yearning, towards its height.

When she finally tore her gaze from the arch, Christiana nearly stumbled into a person standing nearby. She was dizzy from holding her head tilted back, and her vision was blinded from looking into the bright pale sky and the arch within it. "Hey, Christiana, you want to ride the Sky Rider?"

Christiana closed her eyes and threw out her arm, to find her balance. Someone grabbed her forearm, tugging her back to vertical. "Hey, you all right?"

"What?" she asked, only reluctantly leaving where she had been, high in the sky and wind.

"You want to ride the Sky Rider?"

She opened her eyes and saw that Reymundo had hold of her arm.

Reymundo – called "Ray" by most of the white kids at school – had joined Christiana's class in seventh grade, his one of the many Hispanic families that had settled in the area in the last few years. Ray was gangly and dark, with secretive black eyes and hair that he let get shaggy between cuts. Christiana had hardly ever heard him speak, and had no idea he even knew her name. It occurred to her now that he had very little accent. He was staring at her.

"Ride what?" she asked.

"Look," he said, pointing at the nearest building. It turned out to be an open shed, with a long list of text painted on the back and some kind of equipment hanging inside. Three or four people were milling about nearby, and a trashy-looking woman was standing behind a table, smoking. "You put on one of those harnesses and hook on to the cable, and they pull you up to the top of the little one. Then they cut you loose and you fly." There was a note in his voice that made Christiana's throat tighten in sympathy. "But it costs fifteen dollars, and you have to have a partner." He was still holding on to her arm, and he turned his eyes from the arch to her face. "Do you have any money?"

"You mean, we can go up..."

He looked at her intently, then dropped her arm and said, "Yeah. Watch."

The people near the shed resolved into two teenagers and a third who was helping them strap into harnesses that looked heavy but not complicated. Christiana could hear the distant jingling of metal clips and catches. The two riders were moving around, looking at themselves and each other, making wisecracks and hamming it up to cover their embarrassment (and fear, Christiana thought, they're afraid of what they're about to do). The assistant escorted them to a platform at the base of the rectangle, where they ascended six or eight steps. He turned them so they faced Christiana and Ray, and checked all the connections and straps again, and fastened the end of a long, long cable to their harnesses in back. He showed them how to lie down on their stomachs, in seats like canvas hammocks, and he clicked a large connector to their seat near their feet.

Oh my God, Christiana thought. Oh my God. She hadn't noticed the cables before; next to the metal arch they were so thin and fine as to be spider silk. They'd disappeared

108

into the hazy air.

Then a machine began pulling the boys in their hammock seats backwards. Christiana understood then that the cable's other end was the top of the arch, at the vertex of the dizzying, breath-stopping arch, and that the line leading from the connector stretched to the center of the smaller, rectangular arch. With faint clicking sounds it drew them up and up. For a long, long minute the boys diminished into the hot summer sky, blending into a single entity, a speck in the middle of a gray-blue eternity.

Click... click... click. And then,

release,

and the boys were let go to fall and fall, screaming and flailing, all their chances riding in the spider-web strand of cable, and the cable smoothly, smoothly took up the slack, entered into the leap, held on, oh it held on to them and gradually their flight made its return swing; then up and out again but not so far, and back, and again and again until finally they were caught by the assistant on the platform and they were earthbound.

"Do you want to go?" asked Reymundo. "Do you have the money?"

"Yes," she answered.

Afterwards, she could not talk about it. Some of her classmates had seen it, or heard about it, or had learned about it from Ray. They asked her, how was that? or, weren't you scared? But Christiana only smiled or shook her head.

For the next weeks, the Sky Rider dominated Christiana's mind. Its image, pale gray yet tensile and strong, was in her internal eye when she ate breakfast and brushed her teeth. She doodled pictures of it along the sides of her school notebooks, and even on her papers to be handed in. At night, she dreamed she was falling, flying to the end of a heavenly cable, swinging out to meet a celestial embrace. She had never felt so interested in anything before, had never understood what it was to be engaged in a process.

Christiana made an unprecedented move while standing in line with the 120 other seniors, blue graduation robes swishing sibilantly, people goofing around with their caps and tassels. Reymundo was six students behind her, and she stepped out of line and looked in his direction. When she caught his eye, she walked to him.

He didn't speak. His gaze on her was calm but distrustful. They had not exchanged a word since their time together in the air, not even when they had returned to earth and been unharnessed. Now the Hispanic boy with whom Ray had been whispering saw Christiana and fell silent.

"Hey, Ray," Christiana began.

"Hey."

"How've you been?"

"Okay."

"I'll be glad to get this all over with, won't you?"

"Yeah."

The boy behind Ray shuffled his feel and bobbed his head. "Yeah, me too, man," he whispered. "Man, I am outta here, like two seconds after they hand me that piece of paper."

Ray still seemed suspicious. The double line of students took two steps forward, so Christiana backed up.

"Ray I was just wondering..."

He was not going to help her out, not going to make this conversation flow easily. He just looked at her and she heard a heavily accented voice hiss, "Who's da white chick talkin' to Ray?"

Christiana stepped closer and asked, "Do you want to go back there some time? To Dennison's, to ride the Sky Rider again?"

Without hesitation, Ray answered, "Sure."

"Oh, great." Christiana smiled. "When?"

"I don't know. I gotta work."

"When are you off?"

"Next week. Tuesday and Wednesday, I think."

"I can go then."

"Okay."

"Okay? Tuesday?"

Ray nodded.

"Do you have a car?"

"Yeah, I can drive."

"Okay. Great. Thanks."

Christiana raised her hand in a salute, and Ray nodded again. The line moved forward, and she went back to her assigned position.

The ride to Dennison's was made in mostly silence. Ray's car was old, red, and dented, but it seemed to run well, and they flew down the interstate at a steady five miles above the speed limit. They were early enough to get a shady spot to park in, and they stepped out in unison. Ray started towards the park entrance, but Christiana Angelinka hesitated. "Aren't you going to lock it?" she called.

Over his shoulder, Ray answered, "That piece of crap? Who'd steal a car like that?"

"Oh," she answered and hurried to close the gap between them. They each paid the entrance fee to a bored girl in a Dennison's Destination uniform, then walked without discussion towards the Sky Rider.

When they were close, they saw that the shed was empty; the rack of harnesses was shuttered and there were no attendants to be seen. Ray stopped walking and stared. Christiana's heart slowed its beating and she paced softly closer.

Up close, she saw a piece of notebook-sized paper on the ground, dampened by the night's dew and molded to the shape of the grass beneath it. Christiana picked it up and turned it carefully, feeling that it would tear at a hasty touch.

Red letters, their edges fuzzed by the moisture, spoke

gently from the soft paper: "Sky Rider Opens at Noon."

"It opens at noon," she called to Ray. She stooped to position the paper on the grass as she'd found it, then returned to Ray's side. They both looked up at the beautiful arch and its metal attendant, clear in the fresh morning sky. Finally Ray turned his head down. He stood blinking and asked,

"So what do you want to do?"

"I don't know." It was the literal truth. Christiana had thought only of the beautiful swing and her flight in it. The fact of the three hours to be filled before she could fly was a gap in her line of sight. She saw where she was now, and she could see perfectly where she would be then, but in between was an emptiness she couldn't visualize; nor, in that moment, could she conceive of how to cross the gap.

They turned and started slowly towards the center of the park, where other people were beginning to be.

"So, we don't have to hang out together," Ray said.

"Okay."

"Although we could," he added.

"Whatever."

"I mean," he said, and stopped walking. After two steps, she stopped too, and turned to look back at him. His dark eyes were steady as he looked at her. "I mean, you probably don't want to hang with a Mexican."

Christiana pulled her mind away from the feeling of being in the Sky Rider, and returned Ray's look. "Does it make a difference to you?" she asked.

He took his time answering. "What would your parents say?"

This time she could smile. "Nothing."

"Yeah, right."

Christiana walked to Ray's side and took his hand. "I absolutely promise you, my parents would not say one thing about me spending time with you. You want to ride a roller-coaster?"

112

He looked at her carefully, as if he were studying a menu written in French. Then he smiled a little in return. "Yeah."

Because they were early the lines were short and they rode almost everything: the Dusty Miner, with the underground tunnels; the SlingShot, that slung them in a circle so they spent half the ride upside down; and the Tower Drop, that gave them a few seconds' view of the city and an approaching cloudbank before dropping them 160 feet to a jolting stop just above ground level.

Throughout the morning, Christiana Angelinka was aware of the approaching noon hour, when the Sky Rider would open. As the minutes ticked away, her anticipation grew. She held her head higher and laughed more easily. She was glad of Ray's company, and tried to pay attention to him, to repay him for bringing her to the park and for helping the morning pass quickly. They bought cups of chocolate-flavored coffee and sat on a bench in the designated smoking area. Ray smoked a Marlboro from the pack in his shirt pocket while she sipped and swung her feet.

"Now I get to ask, what would your parents say if they knew?" she teased. "If they knew you smoke cigarettes, I mean."

"They know." Ray sucked deeply on the cigarette, and let the smoke escape slowly from his mouth and nostrils. "All the men in my family smoke." He flipped the butt into the nearby receptacle. "It's getting expensive, though."

"How many men are in your family?" Christiana Angelinka smiled again, thinking she'd made a small joke, referring to Ray as one of "the men."

He missed it, and answered seriously. "Six. Me, my father, my older brother George (he pronounced it "Hor-hay"), my mother's brother Carlos, his son Jonathan, and my cousin Martín. He just moved in this year."

Christiana was momentarily startled. "That's a lot of people in one house."

"How many in your family?"

Christiana was surprised to feel a bit embarrassed by her family's scanty numbers. "Three, all girls: me, my mother, my grandmother."

"In a house all by yourselves?"

She smiled but ducked her head.

"I'll bet you have a bedroom all to yourself."

She did not look up.

"And a bathroom too?"

"No, one bathroom we all share." She started to add that *that* was a real trial, but she stopped herself. Her grandmother's cosmetics and her mother's collection of prescription drugs crowding all the counters and shelves might not seem much of an impediment to people who did not have enough bedrooms to go around.

"What are you going to do, now you're graduated?"

Christiana looked across the surrounding hedge, trying to gauge the time by the position of its shadow. "I don't know."

Reymundo drained the last coffee from his paper cup, then crumpled it and tossed it after the cigarette. "Yeah, I'm not sure, either."

Christiana looked at him, but did not comment on the difference she realized lay between "I don't know" and "I'm not sure." It had something to do with *nothing* as opposed to *options*.

"What about your job?" she asked, feeling an unusual urge to fill a silence.

"Making pizzas? It's okay, but..." he frowned, and tilted his head, "what I'm really good at, what I really want to do, is work on cars." He glanced up at her - to make sure she wasn't laughing? to see if she was paying attention ? – then continued, "I'm a good mechanic. I keep that old car of mine running good, and I keep my father's and uncle's cars going, too. I made all A's in auto class. I won an award."

When his voice ran down, Christiana said, "So why

don't you get a job as a mechanic? I think they're much in demand."

Ray's frown deepened into a scowl. "The good jobs go to licensed mechanics."

"Can't you get licensed?"

"No."

"Why not?"

He suddenly stood up, and turned to look at her with his hands jammed into his pockets. "Because!"

She was perfectly willing to let it go. She was thinking it must be noon, or nearly so, but she held her smile and looked in his direction and appeared to be listening, a technique she'd perfected in school.

"Because I don't have papers," he said, and it was a taunt, a challenge. *So there!* His shoulders seemed to add. *What do you have to say about that?*

Christiana had no idea what he was talking about. She sifted through her supply of rote answers, but none seemed appropriate.

Eventually he realized her benightedness and added, "Papers. You know? I'm an illegal."

"Oh!" This seemed such a small matter to Christiana as to be invisible. "Can't you write off and get some?"

Ray stared at her for a moment, and then his eyes opened wide and his shoulders dropped back into place. "No," he said, and he smiled at her, directly. "That's not how it's done. Come on, let's go see if they've opened up the Sky Rider yet."

They got there just as the teenaged assistant was taking down the shutters. The trashy woman, standing behind a folding table with a cigarette in her mouth and a neon pink lighter in her right hand, frowned at them as they approached. "We're not open yet," she said, and then coughed raggedly.

"It's noon," Christiana said calmly. Ray stood beside

her, silent as stone.

The woman lit her cigarette, took a deep drag on it, then pulled a cell phone from her shorts pocket. She flipped the phone open one-handed, gazed at it a few seconds, then flipped it shut. "It's going to storm."

"Not for a while yet," Christiana said.

"It's dangerous to be up in the air during a storm. There are liability issues." The woman spoke with a tone that conveyed boredom and an underlying anger, though with what or whom, Christiana could not guess.

"We won't hold you responsible. We'll sign a paper or something."

Reymundo leaned in and said in a deep voice, "We have the money."

The woman looked at them while the cigarette sifted ash on the folding table. Finally she gave in. "Okay, you want to ride, you're gonna ride. Fifteen bucks each."

The assistant strapped them in, running through the litany of instructions in a mumble that no one could have understood. Christiana wasn't interested. Her breath was as short and impatient as the breeze that bumped them as they stood on the pedestal. It was as though a giant dog was nosing them behind their knees and against the smalls of their backs. Above them, the sky roiled.

They lay faces-downward in the sling, and the boy checked their clips and straps again. "Remember," he shouted at Ray and Christiana, "if the wind gets rough up there, don't panic. All it can do is bounce you around some. It's like an extra thrill for no extra cost, ya' know? These clips can't come open unless somebody squeezes 'em and holds 'em open. Okay?"

Christiana nodded, impatient to begin the backwards ascent to the drop-off point.

Their long feet-first climb seemed to go more slowly than she remembered. Maybe it was because of the wind, that nudged and pushed them and made a dull rumble in their ears. Christiana felt an odd, tugging sensation on her face and realized she was grinning relentlessly. She looked at Ray. He was staring straight ahead, but when he felt her gaze on him, he turned his face towards her. His rich, dark eyes were calm, his face still. Christiana thought he looked older. Burdened. But when his gaze met hers, he smiled, at first deliberately, but then, in the face of her obvious joy, more brightly.

Christiana tried to scoot closer to him in their harness. This tightened the canvas's stricture on some parts of her body, but loosened it on others. Her arms, left free (most of the other riders she had observed had held them straight out in front, in a flying Superman pose) could now manipulate some of the clips and hooks on her back.

Ray noticed that she was adjusting the harness on her back. He bent his head closer to hers and shouted, "What's the problem? Is something wrong with the straps?"

She laughed – although he couldn't hear her – and shook her head. Things were just the way she'd imagined they'd be.

Higher and higher, backwards they were drawn. Their bodies were now well off horizontal, their feet preceding them to the metal rectangle's cusp. The wind was settling into a steady force against them, willing them away from the drop-off point. Christiana thought it would give added impetus to their swing away from the rectangle, her flight through the legs of the beautiful arch.

Finally they were there and the cable held them for a dramatic pause before letting them go. For that moment, the wind held its breath and far, far off Christiana heard a crow caw and the shriek of someone on a rollercoaster. She looked again at Ray, and he looked at her and grinned. Then the cable released and they were flying.

For a few seconds, gravity lost its grip on them, and they felt weightless and had no sense of movement. It was as though the whole world down below was suspended while Christiana Angelinka and Reymundo, up in the sky, waited for their next heartbeats.

Then weight returned and grew, and simultaneously pushed and pulled them forward and down, and Ray laughed. Christiana was concentrating on how much time was left, and she twisted in the harness, turning the front of her body towards Ray while working her arms across her shoulders. Her hand pulled at the heavy canvas, needing to reach the clip in the middle of her back.

Her face was now inches from Ray's. He looked at her and then, in the attenuated seconds of their flight, considered, decided, put his right arm around Christiana's body, and drew her to him. He kissed her fully. The whole length of his body kissed hers as the wind drove them forward and time slowed down.

Christiana, her mind completely open to the beauty and immediacy of her ride, was stunned. For the first time, something another human did, had touched her. For the first time, she was vulnerable to the compulsions of desire and communion. For a moment, something fluttered in Christiana's mind, and she thought, "Oh."

At that same moment, her fingers found and released the last safety clip on her half of the harness. At that same moment, they reached the exact end of their forward ride, and they, the pendulum on this monstrous clock, were about to start the swing back. At that exact moment, Ray realized what Christiana's cold hands had done and he stared into her eyes with shock.

He saw the flutter, the unuttered "oh," and he grabbed Christiana and held her, tightly, tightly, but he could not overpower the arch and the wind and gravity together and Christiana flew out of his embrace.

Ray screamed but Christiana did not. She turned her head to look at Ray and she smiled and then she spread her arms and gave all of herself, every iota of her being, to the air.

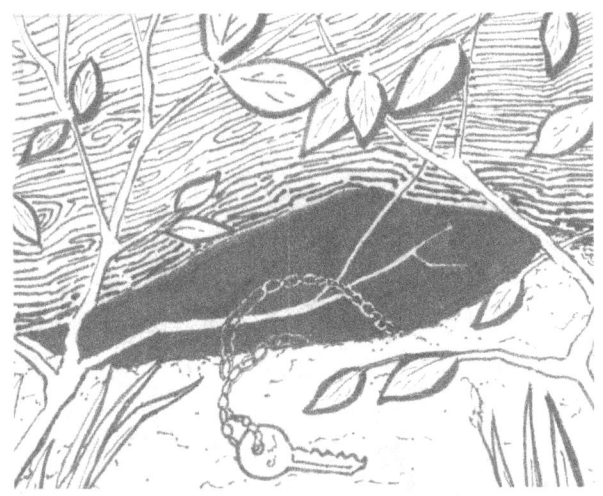

Treasure Hunt

If there hadn't been several pieces of metal shrapnel in that arm, left over from the deceased's tour in Vietnam, Ted never would have found it. It had taken nearly a week of coming out after work, walking around and around the accident site with his metal detector, for what was left of it to come to light. Since the victim had been dead for a couple of weeks before they'd found the other parts of him, Ted didn't figure the extra delay with the arm made all that much difference.

Ted had been a volunteer EMT with the rescue squad for six years, and this wasn't the first time he'd assisted in the retrieval of a body. They had known from the git-go that there was no rescuing to be done on this particular call, but somebody had to haul out the remains, and the squad was the logical choice. They had the equipment and the training.

Somehow Ted had felt bound to go back and make an effort to find the arm. The man's father had come up from North Carolina, and Ted just knew that if it had been his own body that had turned up with one arm missing, his father would have felt better if the arm was found and buried with the rest.

And to heck with certain people's comments that he was only looking for an excuse to use his new metal detector. He'd pointed out to certain squad members that he hadn't known about the shrapnel, but to himself he admitted that he had thought there might be a watch on that arm, so why not use the detector? Ted enjoyed knowing that he'd had the right tool for the job.

The man had been killed when his front-end loader turned over on him. He didn't have any close neighbors. He'd bought sixty-nine acres off the back side of the old Mc-Clure place, and the only way in or out was a little dirt lane he'd bulldozed around the side of the hill. There wasn't even any gravel or shale on that road. It would be bad, practically impassable, in winter, but evidently the man wasn't inter-ested in company and apparently hadn't felt any great need to travel. He hadn't made much contact with people, but he had gotten the word out that he didn't like folks dropping in.

"He was a hermit, that's what," Bobby said, when they discussed the situation over coffee and Mountain Dews, after cleaning out the ambulance.

"Vietnam vet, they all came back crazy as shithouse rats," Fred offered. Fred always had a comment like that, everybody belonged to some group and all the groups were crazy. Ted had personally heard Fred declare that the Ma-sons, the Ruitans, all police personnel, everyone over the age of 60, and anybody who'd work for Sampsons, the only tex-tiles mill still in operation in the whole area, were crazy.

"Who said he was a veteran?" he asked.

"His sister, that's who." Of course Fred had found time to talk up the next of kin. Ted had been too busy using a snow shovel to scoop pulpy body parts out of last year's leaves and into a body bag, to chat.

"Where's she from?" somebody else asked, and Ted was grateful. He wanted to know, but he didn't want to give Fred the satisfaction of asking.

"Down in Carolina. Around Raleigh, near the dad. She

said he'd been a loner for years, but he'd got worse lately. Said they had a deal, he would call them once a week. When they didn't hear for two weeks in a row, they came looking."

"You reckon they found that loader and all?" Ted was refilling his Styrofoam cup from the big coffee urn the auxiliary women kept going, day and night. Darn cups were too little. Just about the time you got it cooled down to where it wasn't so hot it'd take the hide off your tongue and not so cool that it was like sipping dishwater, the cup was empty. Aggravating. His back was toward the men sitting around the table, so he didn't see who asked.

Of course it was Fred who answered. "Oh yeah, they found it. It was them called the sheriff."

"Man," Bobby said, "I'd hate to find my brother like that, two weeks dead and squashed by a loader."

Somebody else ventured, "They seemed pretty calm."

"Well," Fred took control of the conversation again, "they'd been expecting something like this to happen."

"They've been expecting him to get squashed by a front end loader?" Ted asked. He pulled a metal folding chair out from the table so he could sit down. The chair's feet screeched on the linoleum.

"No, not the loader." Fred missed Ted's sarcasm entirely. "Just something. She said he'd been getting worse. Left his wife and daughter a year ago, couldn't nobody figure out why. Wouldn't hardly talk to her nor her dad. Wouldn't have a telephone put in. He called them from a pay phone in town."

"Well, there you go. Miserable man, maybe looking to find Death. Guess he got his wish." Merle. It was Merle putting such a dark color on things.

"Who wants to die alone, like that?" Ted was truly wondering. "If I was looking to die, I would arrange a better way. A man couldn't be sure it would be quick. How would it feel, to lay there with three tons of metal on top of you, knowing nobody would even come looking for days and days?" He shook his head. "I don't believe he was trying to kill hisself."

"Sheriff said there was no evidence of foul play," Bobby offered. He was one of the youngest squad members. He wanted to join the sheriff's department, but he'd heard so much about how hard the police academy was, he couldn't make up his mind to go. But he looked up to Sheriff McKay and his deputies. Hero worship.

Ted sipped too-hot coffee and avoided looking in Fred's direction. "How do you reckon he was getting worse?" he asked nobody in particular.

"Who?" Bobby said.

"If the sister said he was getting worse, he had to have been bad to begin with. What kind of bad do you reckon he was, and how was he getting worse? Like, what were his symptoms?"

Nobody answered, and Ted knew Fred was wishing he could remember something else the sister had said. He was probably sitting there trying to make up something that would sound like maybe the sister, or anybody with some learning, could have said it. Fred hated to lose control of a conversation.

Five days later Ted found the arm and carried it out double-bagged in plastic Food-O-Rama bags. It was pretty far gone, down to mostly bone and some pieces of tendon that shone pearly white among the leaves and black woods dirt. He'd almost missed the shrapnel, but that was what set the detector off, so he'd brushed the litter away carefully until he saw the little gray curls, and he'd brought them out, too. He figured they would help make a positive ID.

On Monday, Ted went straight to the town's maintenance shop, where he was crew chief. He waited for half an hour to see how many of the three-man crew showed up, got them on their way, and then went by the office to see if the Town Manager had anything to tell him. See if anything had

124

broke during the night. Usually, something had.

"Sheriff wants to see you," Sandy said as soon as he walked in the door. She didn't look away from her computer screen. Sandy had worked for the town for 12 years, ever since she graduated from high school. Her job title used to be "town clerk," but last year she'd pestered the Town Council until they'd given her a raise and a new title to go with it: Assistant Manager.

"What about?" Ted waited, but she never took her eyes off that screen. Ever since they'd gotten a grant and upgraded all the office equipment, Sandy spent about one hundred and ten percent of her time with her face lined up with the new 17-inch screen, her professionally manicured nails lined up over the keyboard. At least one member of Council claimed the town couldn't operate without Sandy, but Ted sometimes thought that one of those blow-up dolls, correctly positioned in front of the computer, could accomplish about as much as Sandy. And probably improve morale. His, anyway.

"He didn't say." Sandy squinted, pushed her mouth over to one side, then hit a key three times with her right-hand pinkie, and began to type quickly. That was her signal that she was through talking to underlings, so Ted propped his rear on the edge of her desk and crossed his arms over his chest. He had his own opinion about that.

"What time did he call?" he asked. He kept his tone real light.

Sandy typed for ten more seconds, then sighed and looked through a pile of papers to her left. She came to a pink WHILE YOU WERE OUT message sheet, and read from it in a tone like second-grade teachers use with students who weren't working up to their potential. "Sheriff McKay, 8:01 a.m. Have Ted come by." She laid the note down and turned back to the screen.

"Was it the sheriff himself that called, or one of the deputies?"

"Sheriff," she said, without taking her eyes off the screen.

"Are you sure he was at the office? He didn't want me to come by his house, did he?"

"For pity's sake, Ted!" Sandy dropped her hands, fingers curled into fists, on either side of the keyboard. She exhaled hard, and turned her head to glare at him. "He didn't say, 'come by my house.' He said, 'come by here when he gets in.' I assumed he meant the office. Otherwise he would have said, 'come by my house,' or by the Star, or where ever the hell he wanted you to come."

Ted didn't try to hide a smile. "Okay," he said sweetly. "I was just making sure." He raised himself from the desk and turned for the door, but he added, "Does Jim need to see me?"

"I don't know. Why don't you ask him yourself? Or do you want me to do that for you, too?"

"Why don't you just find out for me, Sandra?" He knew very well that she hated her real name. He'd listened to her telling that lawyer who'd moved into the Greenwood house that Sandra was her grandmother's name, but Sandy sounded more like her: young, quick, of this generation.

Sandy stood up. Her nice new chair, the only one in the whole office that had rollers, went sailing across the floor toward the rear. "Jim!" she shrieked. "Ted wants to know if there's anything he needs to take care of!" Ted took note of the flush crawling up Sandra's neck and deepening her cosmetically blushing cheeks as she went after her chair.

A loud creaking signaled Jim's rise from his third-decade-of-use chair, and he appeared in the doorway of his office.

"Jesus Christ, Sandy," he said mildly, "you don't have to scream. I'm not deaf." He pronounced it 'deef.' Jim was a country boy and didn't care who knew it. He also was a good manager, with an easy way with the workers and a knack for grant applications. He turned toward Ted. "Hey," he said.

126

"Whatever broke last night I ain't heard about yet. You going up to the sheriff's office?"

Sandy blew her breath out hard. She never understood how everybody always seemed to know the business of "her" office, no matter how hard she tried to keep it secret.

"I reckon. You need anything from up there?"

"Nah. But would you tell him he's invited to supper at my house tonight? Betty's frying chicken." Sheriff Duane McKay's wife had died several months earlier, and folks were still trying to take care of him. People think a man can't get along by himself. Sometimes Ted had the same opinion.

"I'll tell him. After I talk to him, I'll start mowing around the courthouse. This may be the last time, this year."

"Be all right with me if it was the last time, ever. One job the less. Okay, see ya later."

Jim went back to his office and Ted turned to go out. "Thanks for asking Jim for me," he said to Sandy, but she refused to acknowledge his existence. Ted figured she was aggravated because he'd gotten her riled and because she, too, didn't know what the sheriff wanted. He was still smiling as we went out the door.

There was a stranger sitting in Sheriff McKay's office, a woman dressed in blue jeans and a knit shirt. Ted saw her when he came in the front door, so he turned to go to the break room to wait.

"Ted! Come on in here." McKay yelled.

Ted went in and the woman stood up. She looked straight into Ted's face while the sheriff said, "Ted, this is Connie Davidson. Her brother was the man killed up on the McClure place."

"This is Ted Johnson," he added, and when she stuck out her hand, Ted took it, and found she had a good grip. She held his hand for maybe three seconds, and then dropped it. Not too fast, not too slow.

"The sheriff told me you found David's arm," she said. Nice voice. Not much accent, no pretense. "I wanted to thank you."

"You're welcome. I'm sorry about your brother." He thought he saw a film of sadness form across her eyes, but it cleared up quickly.

"Would you mind going back out there, and showing me exactly where you found it?' she asked.

Ted glanced at the sheriff, who raised his eyebrows a fraction of an inch, then quickly lowered them. Connie's gaze didn't move from Ted's face.

"There's nothing to see out there," Ted said slowly. "It all looks the same, woods on a hillside."

"I know, but I want to see the place."

"I need to work," he said, even more slowly. He wasn't sure why this woman wanted to see the place where her brother's severed arm had been dragged by nature's clean-up crew, but it didn't seem like a good idea to him.

"I'll wait till you get off," she said calmly. "Do you finish at five?"

Ted glanced again at McKay, but he got no help there. "Usually," he said. "Unless something breaks."

"Should we meet here, or some other place?" She was nothing if not determined, Ted thought.

He hesitated, then said, "I'll meet you at the Star. Four-thirty, okay? "

"The Star?"

Sheriff McKay stepped to the window and pointed out and down. "The Star and Stirrup Diner," he said. "Right down there."

She glanced out, then nodded. "Four-thirty." She settled the strap of a big black bag of some kind, like a cross between a purse and a duffel bag, Ted thought, over her shoulder. She stepped past Ted toward the door, but she turned back just long enough to look him in the eye again, and say "Thank you." Then she left.

He gave her enough time to get out the front door and out of earshot, and then Ted said, "What's going on with
128

her?"

Duane sighed and rubbed his hand across the back of his neck. "Darned if I know. She was here when I got here this morning, waiting in her car till I unlocked. Came in and asked who could show her the place where her brother's arm was found. I tried to talk her out of it, but she is absolutely sure she needs to see that place." The sheriff sighed again and looked out the window. "Hell, I don't know. Maybe it'll bring her some peace."

Ted was quiet for a minute, while he looked the sheriff over. Duane had lost weight in the last year, most of it while he was trying to take care of Nancy at home. He looked a little tired, but not too bad, all things considered.

"You doing all right?"

"Oh yeah, I'm fine." They both waited a little, both hoped the other wouldn't say anything else. After an appropriate pause, Ted said,

"Well, let's go to work. "

"Crimes are waiting to be solved," the sheriff said.

"There's crime in Highlands County?" Ted provided a straight line.

"No, but if I say that often enough, people keep electing me."

Ted walked out of the office but stuck his head back in to say, "Hey. Jim said for me to tell you Betty is frying chicken tonight and she's saving a piece for you."

"I reckon I can handle that," Duane said, with a quick look up.

At 4:30, Ted pulled open the door of the diner. It faced west, and the afternoon sun warmed the air in a long rectangle that lay like a rug behind the counter stools. Ted was still standing just inside the door, waiting for his eyes to adjust to the dimness, when Connie Davidson appeared at his side. "I'm parked around the corner," she said. "We can take my car."

Ted followed her without answering. She led the way to a ten-year-old Chevy Blazer, and Ted had a chance to notice that while she was a little on the heavy side, the jeans looked pretty good. She walked fast and firm, not like she was aware of him behind her.

She unlocked the passenger door, then crossed around the front and unlocked the driver side. By the time Ted was in she had the motor going and was checking the rearview mirror before pulling into the street. She glanced at him.

"Please buckle your seat belt. Family rule. No belts, no go."

He fastened the shoulder belt without comment. There would have been no power in informing her that he always buckled up.

She drove well, calm and quick but without speeding. They spent the first five minutes in silence. Then he asked, "Do you remember how to get there?"

"Yeah. I'd been there three or four times before." Silence threatened to settle in permanently, but she held it at bay by saying, "I appreciate you going back out there with me."

"No problem," he said, although it was, a little. "You've got a key for the gate?" he asked.

"Yeah," she said.

Ted didn't like not speaking to a woman with whom he was sharing the front seat of a car, but he couldn't think of anything to say that wouldn't seem nosy. He was wondering whether he could turn the radio on, when she said, "I got David's key. It was on a ring with a bunch of others, in the loader's ignition."

"Oh."

He was still looking in her direction, watching her chewing on the inside of her bottom lip, when she said, "You're on the rescue squad, aren't you?"

"Yes." From her tone he knew another question was

130

coming, and it was almost bound to be for information about her brother's body. He'd just as soon not go there, for her sake and his.

"You were out there that day?"

He knew what day she meant. The day they scooped up her brother. "Yes."

"Did you know everybody who was there?"

This was not the direction he'd expected her to take. He thought about it for a minute, both to figure out where she was headed and to try to remember who and all had been at the scene. "Probably."

She frowned, but without taking her eyes off the road. "Don't you know everybody on the squad?"

"I know the squad. Know the deputies and sheriff too. I know a lot of people, but I can't remember for sure who else was there. Reporters from Roanoke? There was a piece in the Roanoke paper the next day." He looked at her and saw that this was a serious thing for her, so he added, "Sorry." He was, too. Eight hours ago he hadn't known this woman existed, and he was already trying to keep from disappointing her. He was such a pushover.

Because he hated being a pushover, he asked something nosy. "Why?"

But by then they'd reached the turn they had to take to get to her brother's land. She negotiated the intersection, waiting in silence while a tractor-trailer rig loaded with logs thundered past and made the Blazer rock in its mechanical wind. She didn't answer him while they covered a slow two miles of gravel road. When they got to the driveway, she stopped the car and turned off the engine, but Ted didn't offer to get out and open the gate. She had the key and she still hadn't answered his question, so she could darn well get the gate herself.

Afterwards, she drove very slowly around the hillside. Ted's attitude softened as he decided it wasn't all due to safe driving habits. She might not be thrilled to be there, but she surely was determined.

When they were even with the site of the accident, she stopped the car and turned off the engine. They sat for a few seconds and then she said, "I suppose the place where you found -" the hesitation was barely noticeable "- David's arm was below the road, on the same side as the loader?"

He sighed. "Yes." He didn't make a motion toward getting out of the car. He wasn't going to push this thing; let her make it happen.

"Below or above the loader?" She was looking straight ahead.

"Below."

"Will you remember the exact place you found it?"

"Pretty near."

"How near?"

"Within two or three feet."

"All right then. Let's go." Connie unbuckled her seat belt and opened her door. She set one foot on the ground, then turned to look at Ted. He hadn't moved at all, but when she turned back, he looked her full in the face and lifted his eyebrows. She knew what he was waiting for.

She tried to stare him out, but she lasted only a few seconds. Her eyes dropped to her left hand on the steering wheel. "I need to do this," she said.

It wasn't much of an answer. Ted still wasn't sure whether he was hurting or helping this woman, but he guessed the decision was hers to make. He climbed out of the car and crossed to her side. Together they walked over the narrow shoulder of the driveway and entered the woods, heading downhill.

He made a wide detour around the place where the loader had pinned her brother to the forest floor. She seemed content to follow him and to not look around too much. If she had looked, she would have seen the yellow machine, upright now because the squad had pulled it off the body, waiting among the trees like a big sleeping insect,

132

a hornet that Ted had the sudden idea might wake up and impale somebody again.

He glanced at it to keep his bearings, and led the way thirty, forty, fifty feet below it. There was a hump in the hillside there, a small shoulder that stuck out to create a six-foot cliff, and he walked below the cliff and then stopped. From there, the loader was out of sight. He pointed at a spot ten feet or so back up the hill. If you knew how to look, you could tell that the leaves had been messed up, there. A three-foot wide oval had been cleared, and had not been completely re-covered.

"Right there," he said, and dropped his arm. She looked and then walked slowly to it, going straight to the spot and standing there with her back a little hunched. She took a deep breath - even from where he stood, Ted could see her shoulders rise with it - and sank to her knees. Ted thought she was going to pray, but then he saw that she was sorting through the leaves, running her hands through them to the moist dirt below, starting to circle around the place where the severed arm had lain.

He walked quickly to her side. "What are you doing?" he asked, and none too kindly, either. "What are you looking for?"

"Nothing," she said, but she kept on looking for it anyway.

Ted stood, perplexed and aggravated, while she sifted through another square yard of litter. Finally he loaded his voice with sarcasm to keep his pity from showing, and he said. "Don't you think I brought out all of his arm that was left?"

She didn't answer, and she kept working through the dead leaves and twigs. Ted decided that enough was enough, and he started for the car, but then he saw that her eyes were closed. It looked like her teeth were clenched. He turned back.

"Lady," he said, "what are you doing? There's nothing

of your brother left out here now."

"It's got to be here," she said, and she kept right on digging.

"No, it's not," Ted said. He made up his mind to make her see reason. "Don't you know the animals and insects have done their job by now? Don't you know that he's all gone?" He took a step closer and leaned in toward her. "He's all gone."

"I know that!" she shouted, and jumped to her feet, so that Ted had to step away to keep out of smacking distance. She looked healthy and she had that strong handshake. He didn't feel sorry enough for her to let her vent her troubles by punching him.

"Well then, what?" he roared back at her. He roared because he was, if the truth be known, a little scared of her. Also, curiosity was worming around inside of him. "What are you looking for?" he shouted.

"Well!" she said, as if she was going to jump his case for real. But her tone softened when she added, "Well," and he could barely hear her as she mumbled, "Shit."

When she didn't continue, he said, "Shit won't last out here. Goes in three or four days, tops. If that's what you're looking for, forget it."

She looked him in the eye again then, and after seeming to consider what he'd said, she snorted - which he considered a very unladylike sound - and said, "I know that. I wasn't literally looking for... manure."

Ted thought it was funny that she could say "shit" in the heat of a moment but wouldn't use it in conversation with him. He stood up straight and crossed his arms over his chest. He positioned his feet comfortably on the hillside. He was going to stand right there until she answered him.

She read his body all right, but she still had to think it over before she gave in. "There was something, a little.. thing. A knickknack kind of thing. He kept it with him all the time. It wasn't with the rest of the stuff. I asked the funeral people,

134

but they didn't receive any materials. I asked the sheriff. I even called the crematorium."

Ted hadn't known they'd had the body cremated. Made sense, though, with as little left as there'd been.

"I wanted to ask somebody from the rescue squad, but I was afraid I'd make them mad, and be less likely than ever to get it back."

"You mean you think somebody stole this knickknack." Ted's voice was cold.

"I don't know whether somebody stole it or not, but it wouldn't be the first time possessions were 'lost' during an ambulance ride. Happens a lot, down in the city."

Ted kept his voice steely hard, but there was a tiny acknowledgment inside him that such things did happen. "It doesn't happen up here." Well, not often. "Up here we're helping our families and neighbors. Nobody steals from family."

"Yes, but David wasn't a member of your family, was he?" Her voice coarsened with emotion.

Ted wondered which part of that statement upset her, but he said, "Nobody on the rescue squad stole a knickknack from your brother."

"How can you be sure?" she asked, but he just looked at her. "What if it was something small, something that might, that might ... that somebody might think could get them some money or something?"

He waited.

"It was a key," she finally admitted, in a small voice. "A little brass key."

At last. Ted let a couple of ticks of the proverbial clock go by, then uncrossed his arms. "How big?' he asked.

"Little," she added without looking up. "Two inches long, maybe."

"Not a door key," he said. She didn't speak. "Not on the key ring." She shook her head. He stepped to the top of the little cliff and sat down on its edge, putting his back toward the big metal hornet. She paced around on the hillside for a few minutes, but when he continued to contemplate, she sat down in the leaves. Knees up, elbows on knees, forehead on her crossed wrists.

"Couldn't it be in his house, and you just haven't found it?" He assumed that if she was even considering sifting through forest debris, she'd already gone through the house.

"He kept it with him at all times," she said.

Ted thought some more. "In his pocket? Pants pocket? Shirt pocket?"

"I don't know," she muttered into her arms.

"Then how do you know he kept it with him?"

"He told me."

"He told you it was with him during every waking moment?"

"No, he said 'at all times.' At all times, not just when he was awake. David was so paranoid, if he said 'at all times' he meant he had that key with him 24 hours a day, every day."

"What about when he bathed?"

"He said, 'at all times.' I think he meant exactly that."

"So, he wasn't carrying it in his pockets or his wallet. He probably had it on a chain or something. Maybe around his neck, like dog tags."

"Yeah, I thought of that. In fact, he was wearing his old dog tags when he died. Somebody turned them in. I kept thinking that if the key had been with the tags, and somebody found them, maybe they took the key off and kept it, but turned the tags in. There wasn't a chain or anything, just the two tags. And no key."

Ted sat on the knoll and looked at the woods around him. If he concentrated too hard on the problem of the lost key, he would block the answer. He knew from experience that his mind would continue to study if he took his conscious self out of the process. He would just sit here and

136

watch the evening settle over the hillside, just watch how a few leaves had loosened from their parent trees and were settling onto the ground. He would not get too caught by the smell or the looks or the feel of these woods because that could interfere with his mind working on the other problem, too.

Another thing he had to not think about was Connie Davidson. It was amazing how the image of that woman was in his head, waiting for him to check her out more carefully. Right now, for example, if he turned his eyes to her as she sat in the leaves on the hillside below him, the slow cogitation of the problem of the key and all thoughts of the pretty woods and the changing seasons would be wiped away. Every other thought would be halted by his consideration of whether her eyes were dark solid brown by nature or by contact lens.

He couldn't think about that. He had to just relax and let part of him figure out what would happen to a little brass key in the woods, a little brass key that was close to a big dead carcass, a carcass that was beginning to stink. Stink would have drawn certain animals, birds, insects. Flies and maggots, of course, and rats and eventually even a raccoon or skunk, fox. Not many animals could afford to turn down what was offered to them. Nature could be a skimpy cook, and for some creatures this would have been a feast. Eventually the buzzards would have come, and when they came down they would have scared away the others. The rats would have abandoned ship, as rats do. Rats are smart, first in and first out, usually.

Ted stood up and dusted the seat of his pants. "Guess we'll go," he said.

She hesitated, then stood up too, and turned to slowly survey the hillside. Ted thought her face looked bleak, but she didn't look broken.

"I'll ask around, see if whoever found the dogtags remembers anything else with them," he said, and was pleased that she finally turned her gaze on him. "Then, if you want me to, I'll come back with you on Saturday. I've got a good new metal detector that might help."

Saturday turned out fine, and Ted and Connie were in the woods as soon as the mist had burned off. Ted took the new Fisher 1266-XB out of its case and locked the pieces of its handle together. He took hold of the padded grip, and the machine rose to meet his arm, balanced, with the grip acting as a fulcrum to the weight of the loop. Together he and Connie walked down the hillside. This time they went straight to the side of the loader.

He kept busy, moving briskly and explaining to her what he was doing. He set the discrimination mode for man-made metals and the depth for surface hunting.

"It's harder to find objects that have not been buried long," he explained. "People think it should be the other way around, but what happens is, the longer something is buried, the more direct contact the metal makes with the soil. It starts to oxidize, and the electrical conductivity of the soil around the object is increased. The machines pick it up easier. In a way, the hardest things of all to find are things that are on the surface, that have only been laying out there for a few days."

He didn't look at Connie's face, but he caught the sag of her shoulders. He didn't stop to encourage her. It would be hard; they'd have to be darned lucky to find this key. He wasn't much to hand out hugs and pats, anyway. Not like some of those back-to-the-landers who'd moved in during the '80's: long hair and one earring, always hugging each other.

Ted began the search, starting as near the exact spot where her brother's body had laid as he could pinpoint. He searched a four-by-six-foot section, then turned around and searched the four-by-six next to it. He worked carefully and slowly, mentally gridding the whole hillside and moving from section to section in order, meticulously covering every square foot of ground.

At first she stood just outside the search area, listening to the hums and blips. Every time the potentiometer crackled, her eyes flew to Ted's face, but Ted knew the mineral content of the area and he didn't even slow down for the background jitters. After an hour, she moved to the fallen log and sat down.

He worked straight through till nearly noon, then stopped and removed the detector, flexing his right arm and straightening his back. He'd covered most of the cleared area where Davidson had been working. There had been one or two blips, but they'd uncovered only an old "church key" bottle opener and a fifty-cent piece.

She had walked back to the car and carried out the cooler, and they sat together in the shade of a red oak and chewed on the sandwiches they'd bought at the Star. He ate his with real appetite, but she mostly tore hers apart.

"How powerful is that machine?" she asked.

He gazed ahead while he chewed, then sipped lukewarm coffee from the lid of his thermos before answering. "It's about as good as they get."

"Would you have found it if it was where you've looked?"

He hated to consider how the question stung his pride. "I reckon," he answered succinctly.

She laid down the mess she'd made of the good ham and cheese on whole wheat, took a sip from her Coke, and said, "We're not going to find it, are we?"

He chewed, baloney and cheese on a white bun, lettuce and tomato and onion and a lot of mayo. Extra salt, too. You gotta take some risks in this world, and Ted figured he wasn't carrying much extra weight. A good sandwich was worth it.

He took two or three more bites, then wiped his mouth and said, "I haven't given up yet."

She'd picked up a small stick and was gouging the ground in front of her.

Ted pushed the wrapper from the sandwich and his napkin into the paper bag they'd come in, took one last sip of coffee and then shook the remains onto the ground at his side. He screwed the cup back on top of the thermos, and tore open the wrapper of a Snickers bar.

"Just what does this key open?" he asked. It was plain nosiness, but he'd donated a whole morning plus the other afternoon, and he deserved something for his efforts.

She pushed the little stick in and out of the soft black dirt. "I don't know."

"What?" He was astounded. This wasn't what he'd expected her to say, at all! "You don't even know what it unlocks? Then why are you in such a goldarned rush to find it? You think he's got money stashed away?" Ted had figured that if he found the darned key for her he'd be in on the great unveiling, and now it looked like he was only hunting for a memento, a keepsake of a dead man he'd never met.

She kept jabbing the stick. Didn't look up.

"Well, shit," he muttered. That made her shoot a glance his way, so he added, "Oh, excuse me. Manure."

"Did you think I was looking for money? Did you think you'd get part of the haul?" She sounded like she was accusing him of robbing old people's mailboxes.

Nothing like a little guilt to make you accuse right back. "Did you think I wouldn't help unless I thought there was money involved?"

"Well," she said. Her cheeks were a little red.

He stood up, unrolled the paper bag and stuffed the candy bar wrapper in. "Lady, what I don't know about this situation is just the location of a little brass key. What you don't know would fill an encyclopedia." He started away, and she stood up.

"Hey, listen," she said. "Hey, I'll pay you. I mean, I was always going to pay you, but I'll pay you more now. I mean -" She stopped and huffed a little, then tried it again. Ted kept walking. "Hey, wait a minute. Will you wait just a minute?"

Ted stopped and turned to look at her. She looked him square in the eye and said, "I really need to find that key."

"It won't bring him back," he said.

She flushed, but held her ground. "It's not for me."

Ah, he thought. Boy and his father, on bad terms for years, little sister is hoping for reconciliation from beyond the grave.

Still looking straight at him and lifting her chin a little, she said, "He's got a daughter. He always said that the key would unlock all the secrets of his past, that it would explain everything. She's going to want to know, some day. She deserves that key."

He held her gaze for a few more seconds, then turned and walked in the direction he'd been going. He went to the car and opened the back door, took extra battery packs out of the case, traded them for the two in the detector, snapped down a couple of lids.

Now that the easy work was done, they'd start the real search.

He returned to the wreck site and stood still, looking around the hillside, trying to see the deeper lay of the land. He tried to ignore the mess made by the loader, and to see the more subtle swags and rises. He tried to think of it the way a small animal would think of it: a world where only the low-lying stuff mattered, a place where a rivulet would be a raceway, where an arching root would be a hidey hole.

He walked down to the little cliff where he had found the arm and Connie had begun her search. He fiddled with the controls of the metal detector, and he went over the ground on and near the ledge. He doubled and tripled the scans, moving very slowly and adjusting the controls over and over again. He listened intently. She watched from near the loader.

Eventually he went back to the crash site, looked

around, and headed for an overturned tree.

It had been a massive maple, with a wide and generous spread of limbs that had finally overpowered the hold its roots had been able to make on the slope. When it fell, it tore up nine or ten square yards of soil. Its crash had taken four other trees with it, and had carried limbs from three others. The tangle of saplings and brambles that had taken advantage of the increased sunlight had created a miniature thicket in the midst of the lighter woods.

Ted went to the fallen tree and began another intense search. Back and forth, back and forth. He waved the coil over the ground near the old tree trunk, working through the brush and tangle. He stuck it deeply in, so it was near the massive trunk.

He worked his way from the mass of roots, that stuck up in the air higher than Ted could reach, down one side, then circled the moldering crown and started up the back. On this eastern side of the hill the light was beginning to fail, though clear, strong shafts of sunlight still struck the opposite hill.

Connie had followed Ted around the tree, and had watched closely as he'd poked into every shadow and niche. He could tell she was tired and he was aware when she stopped watching, sighed, and gave up. It was in every line of her back and hips - which he told himself he ought not to be watching so closely. But they were nice hips.

He was minutes from quitting for the day. He'd had a more realistic idea of whether they could find a little metal key in the midst of a forest, and a better appreciation of how long it would take if they ever did find it. But truth to tell, Ted was tired and disappointed, too. It would have been nice to have plucked up the key and handed it to her, to act casual as he accepted her admiration and gratitude for a difficult deed well done. A little of the knight -in-shining-armor business could have made Ted's store operate at a profit, sure enough.

He was on the verge of turning the detector off, of removing the headset and calling it a day, when the audiometer spoke to him. He moved the coils back and forth until he honed in on the source of the response.

It was faint but consistent, a hit when he held the coils right next to the downed tree trunk.

Ted took a step back and studied the location of the hit, marking it exactly in his mind. His fingers tingled with the desire to start pulling weeds away from the spot - or maybe it was because he'd held the metal detector all day - but he glanced up and took note of the darkness settling over the hillside. It would be better to come back another day than to risk overlooking the find in the dark.

"What? What are you looking at?"

He hadn't heard Connie come back to the search area, and Ted tried to cover his start by starting to dismantle the detector.

"Are you giving up?" she asked. She tried to keep her tone neutral, but Ted heard the underlying sadness.

"That's it for the day," he said. He should have stopped right there, but he wanted so much to straighten the line of her shoulders that he added, "I heard a little something. We can come back in the morning."

"You heard a little something? You mean you got a signal from your machine?"

He nodded, but kept his hands and eyes busy with the detector.

"You mean there's something there? Something you didn't dig up?" He didn't respond, which she took to mean 'yes,' and she started to get excited. "Well, why not? "

"We'd have to dig it out," he started to explain.

She didn't wait for any explanation. "Well, let's get to it. Do you need the shovel? The trowel? Show me where, I'll start."

"Now, wait a minute," he began, but she was sorting through the hand tools, picking out a little shovel and a long-handled one. "Wait a minute!" he yelled. She looked up at him but didn't put the tools down.

"It's late and I'm tired and - "

"Okay, fine, you go sit in the car and I'll dig. You've worked all day while I've set around. It's my turn. Just show me where to start and I'll get at it."

"No you won't." He was getting exasperated.

"Yes I will."

"No, you won't! Damn it, woman, will you let me finish -"

"No, you let me finish. You've worked all day, you've done a good job and I appreciate it but now I'll take over and you can rest while I -"

"Will you hush one minute and let me explain something?" In the sudden silence, he could hear his own breath whooshing through his nose. "I'm not so worn out I couldn't dig, but it has to be done right. You just go tearing into there, you're as likely to cover up anything as to expose it. Think of how little a thing this key is. Think of how dark it's getting. Think, Connie."

He should have stopped right there, but he couldn't resist adding, "If it's there, it's probably been there for a while. It's not likely to go anywhere tonight."

It was the "likely" that gave it away.

"Likely?" she said, and she turned her head just a little. "You think maybe it has been moved around, could be moved again? What would have moved a key from one place on a hillside to another, and then just left it?"

She looked at him until finally, in the saturating darkness, he answered, "Rats."

A full minute went by, and when she finally spoke, it was with simple curiosity. "Rats?"

"Rats like shiny things," he said as he bent over the detector again. "You ever dig out a rat burrow, you'll be amazed at what they've drug in there. Tinfoil, paper clips, coins, bottle caps. Bullet shells." He'd found gum wrap-

144

pers and even, once, a whole crumpled pie pan, the aluminum kind that frozen pies came in and that people hung up around their gardens to keep deer out. "Rats will carry shiny stuff in and keep it for a while, then drag it out again. You can bait a rat trap with aluminum foil and get as good results as you can baiting it with food. One time I baited a trap with foil and the next day when I checked on it, the foil was gone and a gum wrapper was in its place. The rat traded. They do that."

Connie stood still for a few more seconds, while he finished gathering up the parts of the detector and then stood up, ready to head up the hill. She didn't move so he waited and eventually she said, "So a rat found David's body and the key, and after eating his fill, it dragged the key off to its burrow. A prize, like the plastic ring in the box of Cracker Jacks."

Lord. Ted set the detector down and walked down to where she stood. "Connie," he said, "Don't think about it. Don't think about that part. I don't really know, anyway. Maybe there was a rat or maybe there wasn't and maybe the key rolled away all by itself or when we moved his body or maybe he didn't even have it on him that day. He could have hidden it and we'd never find it, never. It was just an idea I had, another way to look for the key."

She turned her face away but she held on to the shovels. "It's been over a month," she said. "What if the rat gets tired of the key and drags it out to trade. Maybe it's in there now, but won't be in there tomorrow. We'd never know."

Ted couldn't think of anything to say except, "It's getting dark, Connie. What if we missed it?"

"So if we dig now we might miss it, and if we wait till tomorrow it might be gone."

"I reckon that's about the size of it."

They stood on the hill. In the gathering darkness Ted could see the sky overhead and the outlines of the trees against it, but he couldn't tell the color of Connie's eyes.

145

"I've got a good flashlight in the car," she said softly. "I wouldn't be able to sleep, wondering."

Truth of the matter was, Ted wouldn't have slept, either. "Okay," he said. "Go get it, and I'll stay here and keep an eye on the spot."

She walked away without another word.

The flashlight was six-volt. Ted was glad she hadn't turned it on to make the trip back to the site, and he warned her that once they started using it, they would be blinded to anything that went on around them. "Right here," he said as he knelt at the side of the log. "You stand at the side and shine the light down right here, and help me watch. Watch for little glints and reflections."

She did as he asked, and as soon as she tuned on the light, Ted could see that there was a run, a small covered pathway hollowed out among the grasses and weed stems that grew thickly around the old tree. He put his hand in it and slowly pushed until his hand was swallowed up by the passage, and then began to push the tunnel roof aside with the hidden hand. Before he lifted the weeds, he searched carefully along the floor of the tunnel, feeling with his fingertips for the smooth coolness of metal.

He had bared nearly three feet of tunnel, and his hand had reached the place where the run through grass and weeds was turning down to become a tunnel burrowed under the edge of the tree trunk, when he felt something different. He stopped pushing against the weeds and explored carefully with his hand, staring off into the dark outside the spotlight of the flashlight.

"What?" Connie whispered. Ted had noticed before that being in the dark outdoors always inclined people toward whispering. "What's the matter?"

He frowned, but concentrated on the thing he was feeling, something long and thin and flexible, but not a weed stem. He pulled on it, and it came toward him.

"Have you found something?"

146

He shook his head as he continued to work the thing loose from a snag. It felt like a root had grown up through the dirt floor of the run. It had stubs of small rootlets sticking out from it, and the long flexible thing had been caught on these. The rat had probably tried to pull the long thing down the run and into the burrow, but had snagged it on the root. Because he was working to pull it backwards, Ted had more success than the rat. Soon the thing came loose and Ted pulled it into the light.

It was a metal chain, nearly thirty inches long and silvery, its small links making it pour like liquid into Ted's cupped left hand. Neither he nor Connie spoke for a moment. Then she asked,

"Is that what made the metal detector go off?"

"I reckon so." It was right where the ping had sounded.

Time stretched out until Ted pulled himself to his feet and dusted off his pants and sleeves. Connie continued to shine the light at the ground, and now that he stood, Ted's shoulders and face were cut off, hidden in the dark. The only part of Connie that he could make out was the toes of her shoes.

Ted told her that he was sure the run was made by one or more rats, and that it led to the beginnings of a tunnel. Most likely, the tunnel went down to a burrow, maybe deep down. He told her about the up-jutting root, and how the chain had been tangled around it. "Guess Brother Rat tried to take it down to decorate his living room, but he just couldn't get it there." When she didn't respond, he added, "Sorry, Connie."

"Me too," she said, and suddenly she dropped her arm so that the light pointed straight down and darkness crowded in close. "Guess we ruined the rat's evening. Will it abandon this burrow, now that we've spoiled his front porch?"

"I don't know." Ted's back ached from manipulating the detector all day and then bending over the rat's run. "I don't know if they just take off, or if they try to move all their treasure, or what."

"Well," she said quietly, and turned. She started to walk away, dragging the two shovels that she had held propped against her side while Ted searched the run. Suddenly she stopped. "How deep do rats dig their burrows?" she asked.

"Way deep, sometimes. Six feet or more."

"Would your detector have picked up on something buried that deep?"

Ted closed his eyes. Lord, this woman just would not give up. He answered reluctantly because he was worn out and aching and hungry and he was mad at himself because his big idea hadn't panned out and instead of riding in like a knight, he'd grubbed like a garbage man and come up with nothing but one silver chain, just a necklace without the jewel. "No. It wouldn't have picked it up because I had it set for surface depth."

She didn't even turn to look at him. She just stood there, waiting.

"Now listen," he started.

"If we go away now, the rats will start emptying their nest, won't they? They'll carry out all their treasure, right? Because we've disturbed them? "

Ted hung his head.

"I know you're tired." She tried to sound sympathetic, but the excitement was plain as mud. In his heart, Ted groaned, then he made one effort to cut her off before she got too far down that line of thinking.

"That flashlight's going to go out before long," he said. " Then we'll be in the dark, for sure, and it will all be for naught."

"You know what?" she said. Ted groaned again, only this time out loud. Ted's older sister used to start a lot of sentences with that phrase, back when they were kids. It had usually led to a disclosure that Ted hadn't wanted to face.

148

Like that Ruthie Joines, his dearest love-from-afar during the whole year of fifth grade, picked her nose in the girls' restroom at school.

In Ted's experience, the answer to "you know what?" was usually something he didn't need to know but would likely change his world view. It was stuff he'd really rather not hear, just like he was sure he would rather not hear whatever it was Connie Davidson was going to tell him now.

"That chain could have been what the key and the dogtags were on," she disclosed. "David could have kept them around his neck on that chain, just like you said."

When did I say that? Ted wondered.

"If the key was on that chain and the chain and the key both disappeared, and we found the chain down this rathole, then maybe the rat brought the key here too. Only the key didn't get caught on a root. It went all the way down to the rat's living room. Right?

"How about if I go back to town and buy a new light, and maybe get some sandwiches. Coffee? You stay here and guard this place, and when I get back I'll dig up the nest. I'll do it all, I swear, you won't have to do anything but hold the light."

"Lady, I don't even know you that well. How come I am working myself into the ground - I mean, right into the ground! - for you?"

She stopped then, and was still for a few seconds. "You tell me," she said finally, but she didn't wait for an answer. She handed him the light and swore she wouldn't have any trouble getting up the hill to her car, once her eyes adjusted. Ted leaned against the fallen tree and listened to the sound of her feet shuffling through the old leaves until finally it faded into the silence and then, distantly, he heard the car door slam and the engine turning over. The Blazer's lights cut a shaft through the darkness over his head, then disappeared.

Ted slid his back down the side of the tree trunk until he was sitting on the ground, his legs spraddled out in front of him, the flashlight laying on the ground between him and the rat tunnel. He closed his eyes and let his mind cogitate. After a few minutes, he rolled over and picked up the light, then stood up to set the light on the downed tree trunk so it shined down at the rathole. His mind had considered all the angles, and maybe he was as crazy as she was, but it seemed to Ted that Connie might be right about the key being in the nest. He got the short shovel and started digging.

It was in there. The key, along with a lot of other junk and about a million fleas, was in the burrow, more than four feet below the level of the fallen tree. Connie returned just as Ted was getting close to the chamber. The living room, Connie called it, though Ted thought "trash bin" might have been a more accurate label. When the shovel lifted off most of the roof, they set aside their tools and sorted though the contents with their bare hands. They found the key quickly, and just as quickly, they abandoned the site, brushing fleas off their hands and arms.

Connie shined one of the strong new flashlights she'd brought back from town down at the ruined burrow, and said that she almost felt sorry for the rat. Ted saw her eyes narrow and he knew she was remembering how the chain and key got down there, remembering that the animal had probably chewed on her brother before absconding with the goods. "Almost," she said, and walked over and stomped on the remains of the rat's abode.

They sat together in the Star, and Connie poured the silver chain from one palm to the other while Ted turned the key end for end, holding it lightly between his forefinger and thumb, tapping an end on the bar and sliding his fingers down, then turning it over. Tap, turn, tap, turn, while the chain whispered in her hands.

They met at the diner after Ted got off from work on Monday. It had been past midnight when they'd slogged up the hill from the accident site, and they both were too tired to feel more than a grim satisfaction that they'd found the key. Sheriff McKay had informed Ted that Connie spent the remainder of Saturday night and Sunday night by herself in a room at the Quick 6 Motel. There wasn't much that went on in a town the size of Hayden that everybody didn't know about, right down to who was staying at the only motel. Sheriff McKay even knew that Connie had spent Sunday at her brother's house, and Ted hadn't needed the sheriff to tell him that she'd been searching for the lock that the little key would open.

"You don't have any idea what this unlocks," he said. It was the third time he'd said it since they'd set down at the counter.

She just looked at him.

"And there wasn't anything in his house that looked like it had a lock anywhere near that size?"

She looked at him some more, and gave a little snort. He reckoned he deserved it. Any fool would have been trying that key into every hole in the house, whether it was in a lock or in a block of Swiss cheese.

The heavy glass and metal door swished open and Fred Clodfelter walked in. Ted sighed and palmed the key, and began to study the dregs of coffee in the thick white mug in front of him.

Fred climbed onto the stool next to Ted's. "Keeping busy, ole buddy?" he asked.

"Yeah," Ted answered. He stood up and tried to talk like he was just making an announcement to the general world and not specifically inviting the woman at his other side to go with him. "Reckon a trip out to the country might be good about now."

Connie looked up, obviously puzzled, and asked, "Where are you going?"

"Yeah, where you going, ole buddy? I just got here." Fred was looking at Connie with hunger in his little eyes.

He knew who Connie was. After all, he'd spent all that time talking to her while the rest of the Squad had done the dirty work. Now he was eager to find out why she was still in town, and why she was in Ted's company.

Ted tried to signal Connie with his eyebrows as he said, "Well, I just thought a walk in the country might be good. Exercise. Good exercise."

Fred didn't lift his gaze from Connie's face as he addressed Ted. "You ought to be in mighty fine shape, as much walking as you do these days." He smiled so that all of his store-bought teeth showed. " Me and Ted have knowed each other since we was just kids. You might say we growed up together."

"Is that so?" Connie asked. She had leaned back a little and glanced up at Ted.

"Oh yeah. Childhood buddies, you might say. Our wives was even best friends."

Now that amounted to a lie. Ted and Fred had been two of the eight kids that had gone through grades one through seven together at Long Ridge Elementary School, so it was reasonable to say that they'd been friends. Of a sort. The sort that knew each other's family for three generations back and hadn't had much respect for a single member thereof.

But Fred's wife and Melissa had not been friends. One of the few things that Ted and Melissa had agreed on for the entire six years they'd been married was that Fred and Shirley Clodfelter were people with whom they had not wanted to socialize.

"How nice," Connie said. She leaned down to get her purse, then stood up. "Guess I'll take that key," she added, and held out her hand to Ted.

Ted dropped the key into Connie's hand. He opened his mouth to speak, but Fred beat him to it.

"Key? Ya'll been sharing a door?" He laughed to show he didn't really mean it, but the effort failed. Connie looked down at him with a gaze she might have lavished on a clod of manure that had been tracked in and said, "No. Mr. Johnson helped me locate a lost key."

Ted winced at the "Mr. Johnson."

"Oh, yeah, ole Ted is a big treasure hunter. I'll bet he brought out that fancy metal detector he has, and detected that key for you in no time. Yes sir, Ted loves to hunt for treasure. Knows all the tricks, like checking for a loose hearthstone, and looking under front steps and everything. Say, Ted," he said, and looked up with lifted eyebrows, "you know, I heard that a real good place to look for treasure is down in old toilet holes. They say stuff would fall out of people's pockets when they dropped their drawers, coins and pocketknives and watches and all kinds of things. Once it went down the hole, nobody crawled in after it, ya know."

"Yeah," Ted said, and started away. He didn't have to stand there and listen to Fred. Maybe if he moved away, Connie could get out of Fred's line of fire, too.

"And you know," Fred said quickly, loath to let them out of his reach, "another place old people used to hide stuff was under certain fenceposts."

"Is that right," Connie said. She slid off the stool. Ted heard, for almost the first time, a hint of an accent in her voice. She sounded just the littlest bit like a Yankee.

"Oh yeah, always a certain one. Like, the eighth post from the south corner of the barn. It was always the eighth."

"The eighth," she said coolly. Definitely a northern chill there.

"Well, unless the farmer had another number that was special to him. Like, if he had a lucky number, he'd pick that fencepost and bury his treasure in a box under it." Ted said it like it was a fact, plain and simple.

"Fred, where do you get this crap?" Ted had a feeling that part of the chill in Connie's voice came from Fred's comment about wives. He had been married, but he'd also been divorced for eighteen years, but had Fred included that in his little litany of personal history?

"Hey, this ain't crap." Now Fred sounded self-righteous and insulted, the way congenital liars sound when people don't believe them the one time they slip up and tell the truth. "I didn't make that up. Old man McClure told me that."

"Old man McClure hasn't had a logical thought in five years."

"Well, maybe he can't keep people's names straight, but he remembers stuff that happened a long time ago, clear as a bell."

Ted dug his wallet out of his hip pocket, and laid a dollar on the counter beside his coffee mug. Connie was walking out the door and he wanted to catch up with her even more than he wanted to get away from Fred.

"You know that's true," Fred insisted. Now his dignity was hurt. "He told me a lot about the old times, about when cars first came into this country, and about walking all the way to Damtown to work at the mill. He told me that about farmers burying stuff under a fencepost, and it's the truth, sure as shit."

Ted started for the door. Fred, desperate for Ted's interest, said, "You know who else used to listen to Enoch McClure? David Davidson, that's who. That woman's brother used to think Gabe was worth listening to."

Ted threw up his hand as he went out the door. He wouldn't insult a fellow squad member by not acknowledging his departure in some fashion, but he'd be darned if he'd offer a real good-bye. To heck with Fred.

He caught up with Connie before she drove away. He put his right hand on her windowsill, and tried to think of something to say. "Well," was his enlightened opening, "is there anything else I can do to help?"

"No. I appreciate everything you've done already." She studied the instrument panel for a few seconds. "I should have known from the beginning that it was a wild goose chase. I just wanted something to give to Bethany. Something, some piece of her dad."

"I could help you search the house one more time. Maybe a new pair of eyes would notice something you've looked at until you don't even see it any more." Even as he said it, Ted didn't really believe it. But he hated to let this story go before the final scene.

He didn't expect Connie to go for it, but after a small hesitation, she said, "Don't you have to let your wife know where you're going and how long you'll be gone?"

"I haven't had to let her know anything since she divorced me, 18 years ago."

She slid the Blazer into gear. "Then come on. The electricity's been turned off, and the daylight will go quick." Suddenly, Connie's voice was as southern as sassafras.

Ted had never been to the house. It was a small white frame building with overgrown boxwood bushes hiding most of the front porch. There was a new woven-wire fence around the yard, the wire stretched tightly between clean peeled fence posts. Despite that, the place had the look of absence, with curtainless windows, no path of stones or trodden grass to either front or back door.

Inside, it was typical of the place and time it was built, probably in the thirties: wood floors with linoleum rugs in the centers of the rooms; four rooms off a central hallway that led straight back to a bathroom that had been added by taking out a slice of the back bedroom. Stairs up to two bedrooms overhead. Ted would bet those rooms had low ceilings that sloped to waist height at front and back. He'd grown up in a house like this.

For a bachelor's house, it was tidy. Not much furniture and no knickknacks, no pictures on the walls. There was a big homemade bookshelf full of paperbacks with their spines lined up. A big, expensive-looking radio crouched on the top shelf. One big recliner filled up a corner, a floor lamp beside it.

Some guys didn't know how to pick up the empty boxes from their microwave dinners, but this house was neat. Organized.

Ted and Connie walked through, taking it slow so Ted could look it over carefully. He realized immediately that there weren't many hiding places in that house. Upstairs, the old wallpaper had been stripped from the walls, revealing rough poplar paneling. One of the rooms was completely empty. The other contained six medium-sized cardboard boxes, their tops lapped shut.

Ted didn't have to ask about the boxes. Connie said, "I took everything out of every one of them. They're full of books. Paperbacks, mostly science fiction and fantasy."

There was storage space in the back, behind the knee-wall of the upstairs bedrooms. Its emptiness echoed in the spaces between the bars of an old iron bed frame propped against one wall. Ted ducked his head and went inside to look carefully at the exposed rafters, and at the nooks where rafters, roof and walls met. All were bare-faced empty.

The kitchen offered the most possibilities, but there was nothing that Ted could find that needed a key, nothing that could hold treasure of any kind. He went through the motions of opening all the cabinets and looking in all the containers, but there was nothing.

In the failing light he went out and looked in the springhouse, which had been cleaned out and coated with waterproof whitewash; and the old chicken house. It was as empty as the attic had been, with no thick walls to hide a secret compartment and a floor held up on stilts showing that nothing could be hidden underneath.

Connie joined him as he stood in the dusk, looking at the old farmstead. "Come on in," she said. "I brought some coffee."

They went in and sat in the light of a kerosene lamp, drinking coffee out of her Thermos.

After he had listened to the house settling for as long

as he could stand it, Ted said, "This is a nice place."

"Yes. Hard to get in and out of, but it suited David."

"Was he always a loner?" It didn't feel so much like being nosy, now. Felt like he was asking for the right reason.

Connie looked into the corner of the room like she was looking down a long hallway. "No. David was four years older than me, and when we were little, we were just regular kids. We played together for a couple of years, when I was old enough and he wasn't too old. Then he got to be a teenager and he had friends. Guys. He ran track, and hung out with the other members of the track team." She smiled a little. "I was a freshman in high school the year he was a senior. I don't know about where you went to school, but at Pembrook, the track guys and the football players were rivals. The football players were bigger, tougher, always wanted to fight. The runners considered themselves intellectuals. They'd set up big practical jokes for the football team, and the football jocks would raid the track meets, looking to jump on any of them they could catch. They didn't catch them very often."

"Huh."

"David went off to college and seemed to be doing okay. He met Diana, she got pregnant and they got married. He quit school to get a job and support them. Then he joined the Army. We never could figure out why."

"He had a good deferment."

"Oh yeah. And he must have known that if he joined, he'd go to Vietnam. This was in 1970. Everybody was going." She sipped her coffee. "Two tours. He did two tours."

"That was a bad scene."

"Well, he was never the same, but he wasn't as bad as some. He kept everybody at a distance. He and Diana divorced. When she remarried, her new husband adopted the girl and they told David to disappear. Eventually he met Marianne, and they had a child. We thought maybe he'd really settle down, but they never even got married. Biggest thing they shared was a drug habit."

Time ticked by, measured off by the old house cooling and popping gently. "Once, when I was in the ninth grade and seniors were like a higher form of life to me and my friends, Mom and Dad had a birthday party for me. It was awful, because they did it the wrong way, with balloons and a birthday cake with pink and white icing. They even had those stupid little hats, you know, shaped like dunce hats?

"I was trying so hard to be grown up and a *high school-er,* and they had done all the little-kid stuff. My so-called friends were just standing around waiting to leave. I was so embarrassed I would have crawled through broken glass to have gotten out of there. David found me in the hall closet. I had shut myself in the hall closet, and he opened the door and asked me what was I doing. I told him to go away and leave me alone. So he closed the door and went away, and in a little while I started hearing the front door opening and more people coming in, and I could hear voices. Male voices. Finally I had to open the door and look. David had called all his friends and told them to come over. All these senior boys were there at my house, at my birthday party, and all the girls who had been about to label me the biggest dweeb in school suddenly thought I was the coolest person around, and that our house was the best house to hang out.

"He used to take care of people like that. No fuss."

Ted sat and let the night come on. Outside, darkness wiped out perimeters and opened borders. Mysteries seemed to hover at the edge of the lamplight, just out of reach.

"I thought," Connie said, very quiet now. "I thought coming up here meant David was getting better. I thought he was quitting drugs, making a place to live with his daughter. He loved that little girl so much.

"What a waste," she said, and stood up. "Time to go."

Ted carried their mugs to the kitchen and rinsed them. He drank a cupful of the gravity-fed water, and found it cold and clear-tasting. He walked slowly back to the living room, where Connie was standing near the lamp, ready to turn

158

down the wick. Ted realized he was stalling, delaying the time when he'd have to tell this woman good night and maybe good-bye. He stopped to look at the titles of the books on the shelves. They were history books, and after a minute he realized they were arranged chronologically by subject matter. At the top left were books on ancient Egypt , the Phoenicians, Byzantium, Romans and Greeks. Then came a section on Britain: Celts, Druids, King Arthur, William the Conqueror. Lower, the colonization of America, the Revolution, Lewis and Clark. The Civil War, cowboys and Indians. Canals, railroads, steamships, automobiles, airplanes. At the bottom right, a few books about World War II.

Ted pulled a book at random and let it fall open. There was a dog-eared page, and he skimmed it, but hardly registered what he was reading. "The men had no shelter tents, and the weather grew much worse..." Ted flipped forward to another dog-eared page, and read, "This line was strongly manned with first-rate troops." He closed the book: *A Stillness at Appomattox,* by Bruce Catton. A book about the Civil War. He put it back in its place and slid another one out. It, too, fell open to dog-eared pages. He tried a third book, and a fourth.

"Are you finding something?" Connie asked.

"Every one of these books has dog-eared pages," Ted said.

She moved close and looked at the books he pulled out and opened. "I guess he was marking passages that he thought were important," she said.

"Maybe. But look. This one has page 13 marked, and page 113, and page 213."

"So?"

"So did the last four books I checked. Always page 13, and page 113, and 213." He looked through a couple more, and they were marked in the same pattern.

"So, you think that means something?" Connie was puzzled, by the way her brother had marked all the books and by Ted's reaction.

"Thirteen, thirteen. Was there something special about the number thirteen for David?"

Connie replied slowly, giving it some thought, "No, I don't think so. Thirteen's the unlucky number, isn't it?"

Ted tried to let his mind go quiet, to let ideas come without consciously pulling them along. Somewhere lately someone else had used that phrase, "unlucky number." Somebody had told him a story about unlucky numbers... But the memory wouldn't come clear.

Connie turned on a flashlight and blew out the lamp, and she and Ted went out to the Blazer. She drove slowly down the long driveway, and Ted was quiet, trying to let his mind work. When they got to the gate, he got out without speaking and pulled it shut behind the car, working in the red light of the taillights to fasten the chain to the heavy post.

He turned and started back to the passenger side, then suddenly stopped. He stood for a few moments, and then opened the door and got in. Before she could get the car in gear, Ted said, "Connie?"

She turned and looked at him, both their faces barely illuminated by the instrument lights, hanging like question marks in the dark.

"Would you feel like coming back out here tomorrow and looking in one more place, just on a hunch?"

Now it was her turn to sit quietly and consider.

"It would involve more digging," he added.

She pushed the gearstick into first. "Oh well, why didn't you say so?" she said as she started the Blazer toward town. "Digging has become one of my favorite pastimes."

Ted had had a big urge to tell Connie to turn the Blazer around and go back to the house last night, in the dark. But his better sense had prevailed, and once he was actually there again, in broad daylight, with his detector in one hand and his shovel in the other and with Connie standing at his side with a bright, expectant look in her eyes, he was glad he'd waited. Now he was definitely having second thoughts.

"This may not amount to anything," he said.

"Tell me what you're thinking," she asked. "Have you come up with a clue, or are you just going to search all over the yard?"

"No, not all over." He gazed at the house and its encircling fence.

"Well, where, then? And why?"

"It was just something somebody said."

"Did you tell somebody else about this?" she asked, sounding very carefully neutral. Ted had already figured out that Connie Davidson didn't like to have her personal stuff known and talked about by others, not much more than she liked talking about them herself. It was a trait Ted respected.

"No. Wasn't talking about you at all, really. Just general talk. Sort of."

She looked at him and planted her feet. He knew she wouldn't move them until something made it worth her while. Stubborn woman.

"Well. It was Fred Clodfelter." Man, he hated having to drag that name and that image into his conversation with Connie.

"Who?"

"Fred. Fred, from the Star, the other day? He's on the rescue squad too."

"Oh, that man." Very noncommittal, if you didn't notice a certain tone in her voice. At least they agreed on that subject.

"Yeah, well, remember when he was going on about treasure hunting, that day at the Star?"

"Sort of. I didn't pay much attention, really."

You paid attention to the part where he almost said I was married, Ted thought with a hidden grin. "Me either, really. That's why it took a while to sink in, I guess. He said that old people used to bury their valuables under fence posts."

161

"What?"

"Well, it makes sense, if you look at it in the right way. Let's say you've got something that's valuable, but you don't use it. I mean, it wouldn't be money, because you'd want to be able to get at your money every once in a while, right? But what if it was some kind of a thing that meant a lot but you didn't need to have it at hand all the time? Something that was maybe an heirloom. Think of a silver cup. Maybe it had been your grandfather's, or his grandfather's, and you wanted it to be handed down to your kids too, but in the meantime, you were worried about losing it or it getting banged up or maybe even stolen. So you'd hide it. Right?"

"I suppose," she said.

"Some place safe and secret, someplace that might be hard to get at, with maybe a clue that only the people closest to you would find or understand."

She just looked at him.

"The other day, Fred said a real old-timer told him that people used to bury their treasure under fence posts."

Connie looked at the house with its circling fence, and then let her gaze go wider, taking in all the old fencing that marked the sixty-nine acres of her brother's land into pastures and hayfields. She stood quietly and considered.

At least she wasn't openly scoffing at him.

But when she spoke, she shook her head and said, "Ted, I don't think that helps us at all. There must be hundreds of fence posts on this farm. Which one would David have picked? We could dig for months and not find anything but rocks. And besides, I never heard that kind of story before. Had you?"

Ted shook his head.

"But if you hadn't, and I hadn't, then what makes you think David knew it? He wouldn't have had the first idea about burying things under posts, even if we could figure out which one he would have chosen."

"Well, I think David did hear that story," Ted said.

"Fred Clodfelter said he had."

"Now, why would Fred Clodfelter know anything at all about my brother?" She was more than a little touchy about Fred.

"Because the old man that told Fred about burying stuff under posts, said he'd told David too. It was Enoch McClure, and his family used to own this land, and until six months ago, Enoch lived in that little house across from the end of this driveway. He used to walk out here, see what was happening to the house he had helped build when he was young. He told Fred that he'd told David about the posts.

"And besides," Ted added, "I think your brother left clues so you'd find his treasure. He told you it existed, told you to take the key that he figured would be easy to find because it would be right on his body, and then he marked all those books."

She was looking at him hard.

"All those dog-eared pages with thirteens. I just have an idea that David buried his treasure under the thirteenth post, like Enoch McClure told him to."

She looked and looked at the house and all the fences. Finally she said, "Which thirteenth post? The thirteenth, counting from what? Which fence, even?"

"The yard fence, I think," he said. "It's new. He set all those posts himself, within the last year. Maybe while he was at it, he set a box in there too. If it happened to be a metal box, we can figure it out right quick."

Ted leaned the shovel against the gatepost and adjusted the settings on the detector. He walked right from the yard gate, and counted thirteen posts. He had turned the corner and was in the back yard, three posts deep into the garden. David Davidson had kept a neat garden, with three rows of long raised beds, each bordered by grassy paths. From this side, the place looked lived in and loved.

The thirteenth post was near the end of a bed full of the dried stalks of sweet corn. They leaned at odd angles, supporting each other like frail old drunks. Ted aimed the coil of the detector at the foot of the post, and listened carefully as he worked his way around the post. When he got back to where he'd started, he stepped back one step, and made another circuit. He adjusted the meters and tried again. Then he took off the earphones and said, "Nothing."

Connie trailed after him as he returned to the front gate, turned left, and marched along the fence, counting posts. Between numbers four and five they stepped across the spring branch, that rose in the springhouse Ted had looked at the night before. Five was the corner post, and they turned west to follow the fence to the back. The thirteenth post was near the chicken house, under the arms of two tall cherry trees that were dotted with holes in horizontal rows around the trunks. Woodpeckers had been working those trees, gouging holes to get the beetles just under the bark.

Ted glanced at Connie before he began his circuit of the post, but she was looking at the tree on the far side of the small clearing. He watched as she put out her hand and gently touched the old tree's chest, and ran her fingers over the holes.

"They don't hurt the tree," he said.

She didn't speak, but used her index finger to follow a line of holes down, then, from a new starting point, in an outward arc, and a second bulging arc.

"Thirteen," she said.

Ted went ahead and checked with the detector. On the west side of the thirteenth post, the side nearest the marked cherry tree, there was a resounding ping at four feet. They dug slowly. Somehow, now that they were sure they were going to find it, they were reluctant. Ted wondered if she was a little afraid of what they might find. He wondered why he was so unenthusiastic.

It was bigger than he'd anticipated, a metal box nearly two feet square. David had wrapped it in heavy plastic and taped it with duct tape. They lifted it from the hole and Ted shoveled the dirt back in, neither of them rushing to open the thing. They carried it to the back porch, which was sunnier and warmer than the front.

"You want a drink of water?" she asked. He nodded, and she went in to get it. They both sipped spring water from coffee mugs, and he looked around the old place again, noticing how well the land lay, and that there were plum and apple and peach trees on the north-facing hill. There were twelve or fifteen blueberry bushes along the back fence.

"I guess we'd better open this," she said.

"Would you like for me to go for a walk?" he asked.

She shook her head no, and she reached inside the collar of her shirt and brought out the silver chain, and the little key on the end of it. He used his pocketknife to cut away the tape, and helped her fold back the plastic. The key slid in without resistance, and she turned it slowly. Two soft clicks, and she withdrew the key, put her hand on the lid, lifted.

There were big, extra-strong manila envelopes, stacked up so that the top one was at the lip of the box. It had "1948" printed on it, and when Connie opened it, old photographs fell out.

Some were in faded color, many of them were black and white. They were of David and his mother and father, grandparents, cousins. He had been born on March 6, and there were pictures of him in his christening gown, in his mother's arms, propped on a pillow. There were old studio portraits of people in the clothes of an earlier era. Connie looked at one of these and said, "These were our great grandparents, I think." Ted reached out and turned the photo over. On the back, in small, careful letters, someone had written "Lester and Maribell Davidson, Grandfather Samuel's parents. Moved to North Carolina from Boston area, 1854."

Each of the envelopes was labeled with a year or a decade or five years or some other period, each one held the illustrations of a life. "When did he collect these?' Connie wondered, but Ted had no answer. On the back of each photograph he had printed one or two lines of information: the identities of the people pictured, or what the occasion was that had been photographed, or some personal insight about the subject. "Cousin Donnie loved snakes better than women," on one. Connie laughed and said that that was undoubtedly true, since Donnie had never married but had kept pet constrictors in terrariums for years.

There were a few pictures of David's first wife, just one in the packet of a little girl, taken when the child was a toddler. On the back, David had printed, "Diana and Dennis Weaver's daughter, Susan."

"That the daughter from his first marriage?" Ted asked.

"Yes." Connie studied the photograph and said, "It broke my mother's heart that David wouldn't try to have some custody of that child. Not even any visitation. He just gave her up."

"Now you know why," Ted said.

She looked at him with her brows drawn down. "Now I know?"

Ted looked at her and waited for the light to come on. Finally, he said, "What did he write on the back, Connie?"

"'Diana and Dennis Weaver's daughter.'"

"Connie, he didn't say she was his daughter. He said she is Dennis' daughter. I'll bet Diana and Dennis were friends before David and she got married. Weren't they?"

Connie didn't speak, but her eyes told the story. She put the picture back in the envelope and closed it. Set it aside.

They came to the years when David had been in Vietnam, and there were pictures of men in disheveled uniforms, sitting in camp, playing cards, laughing and smoking. There were pictures of Vietnamese villages, and pictures taken during combat. Some were so awful, they could barely look at them. "I think we ought to burn these," Connie whispered.

"What was it he told you the key would unlock? All the secrets of his past?"

She wouldn't look at him.

"He never talked about this much, did he?" She shook her head. "This was one of his biggest secrets. I think he meant for us to unlock it, to open it up, Connie. Maybe save it from his little girl until she's old enough to ask about it. Don't throw it away."

The final envelope was not dated. Connie shook out the thick stack of pictures, and they slid across her lap and into the last patch of sunlight on the weathered porch floorboards. All of them were of a little girl with pudgy cheeks and dark eyes. There were shots of her laughing and crying, of her as an infant and as a toddler and as a little kid with a backpack, waving from the steps of a yellow school bus.

"This is his daughter," Ted guessed, holding a picture of the little girl in the arms of a man with a beard.

"Yep. David's daughter."

"She looks like you, a little. The eyes."

Connie was examining another picture. "Well, she does, doesn't she?"

"Mmm-huh."

"Davidson eyes."

In the bottom of the box there was another envelope, smaller, tied with a red ribbon. Inside was a small blue bankbook, the old-fashioned kind in which withdrawals and deposits into a saving account would be entered by the hand of a bank teller. There were also some sheets of lined notebook paper, folded in thirds.

Connie opened the papers and read them, slowly. Then she handed them to Ted.

Dear Connie,

Since you're reading this, I guess it means something has happened and I'm gone. It means I've failed again, but the good news, Little Sis, is that maybe I didn't get to the end of the tunnel, but I was, finally, going in the right direction.

A lot of my life has been a mess. I don't have anyone to blame but myself. I don't expect anybody to understand or forgive me for the times I've hurt and disappointed them, but I wish I hadn't done it. It was like I got started down a certain road and just couldn't find a turn-around place. There were moments when I knew I was heading for disaster, times when I'd wish I could go back and start on a different route, but mostly I just kept hurrying on toward trouble.

It used to be so easy to be a nice guy. Then, every time I got my feelings hurt I'd pretend like it didn't matter. I'd cover it up. Somehow the hurts kept coming and kept getting bigger and bigger, Diane and then 'Nam and everything, until finally I had pretended so much that none of it mattered, that I forgot how to let anything at all matter.

Until Bethany was born. From the very beginning, she didn't care whether I pretended or not. I always knew she was mine, that no other man would come to claim her, and that even her mother didn't much care about her. And Bethy was so uncomplicated, and so honest. She was just there to love and be loved, and when her love finally got to me, it was big, Connie, feelings like I never had imagined might exist, much less feel.

I would have stayed and taken care of her in Raleigh, but for her sake I had to get rid of the drug habit and the drug scene. As soon as Bethy was big enough to go to school, so she didn't have to depend on her mother for every bite of food and shelter - because I knew it, Connie, that sometimes Marianne might not keep her head together enough to feed a baby, or keep her diapers changed - I found this place and bought it, and moved here and started making a place for me and my daughter.

I was afraid to tell anybody because I knew it would be hard and I wasn't sure I was strong enough. I didn't want to make big promises I couldn't keep. I didn't want anybody to help. I had to do it myself. I told Bethany, I told her about a million times, and I hope she remembers that, because if you're reading this, then I didn't get done.

Sis, it's about as hard to ask this as it was to decide to leave Raleigh and let Beth stay there for a while without me, but I have to do it. I have to do it for my little girl. Connie, would you please take care of her for me? Raising a kid is the biggest thing a person can ever take on, but I believe that once you get to know her you will love her too, and that will make everything a joy. I hope it will. It changed my life, Connie, and the best thing I could possibly wish for you is that you come to love this little girl. But even if you don't, if you never have this connection with her, I know I can trust you to provide for her. I know that at least she'll be warm and fed and clean and educated and looked after. That's all I ask. If you love her, it will be the icing on the cake.

I have been putting everything I can into this place and into the savings account. There should be enough money to send her to college. The place is yours, to keep or sell, whether you take care of Beth or not. There's an insurance policy with American Amicable, not big but enough to cover some things while she's growing up, or whatever. The papers are in the desk at Marianne's, if she hasn't lost them.

That's it, Sis. I'm sorry we missed so many years. I hope like Hell that you never have to read this letter. I think I'm finally getting things straightened out, and I have a good feeling about this farm. I like to sit on the back porch here and watch the dark come on and listen to the bugs and imagine how it will be when Bethy is here and you and Dad come to visit. We could make ice cream in one of those hand-cranked freezers like we had when we were kids.

Remember those long summer evenings when the lightning bugs would blink under the trees and we would play out there until ten or eleven o'clock while Mom and Dad sat on the patio and listened to the radio? Sometimes I *would climb up in that biggest maple and watch all the rest of you playing and eating and fussing and slapping mosquitoes. I used to think that was so wonderful that I couldn't stand to go into to bed and sleep, afraid it would slip away and we wouldn't have the magic any more.*

I guess it did slip away, didn't it? It always does, for everybody, but what I've discovered is, for the lucky ones, a new generation comes along and starts it all over again. For the lucky ones.

Good luck, Connie. Thanks for everything.

He gave the letter back to her and they sat together on the porch while the dark came on and it got cool. A hardy cricket began to chirp under the step, until it got cold and quit.

"Connie?" he said. "Would you let me buy you some supper?"

"I'm pretty tired." Her voice rose softly through the dark air.

He sat for a few minutes more, then stirred and stood up. "I'll get on, then." He reckoned the story was told, but he still didn't want to leave her there by herself. Didn't want to intrude either.

She stood too, pushing up from the floor where she'd been. She put out a hand and touched his arm, just above the elbow. "Thank you very much for all your help. I would never have known..."

He raised his hand and grasped her elbow and held her, as firmly as he could without hurting.

"It just makes me so sad, and... sad." She ended at a whisper, and bowed her head. He leaned forward very slightly, and her forehead touched his chest. They stood like that for a minute, and he thought she might have cried a little. His free hand found hers, and he was glad his was warm. She felt chilled.

"Your brother thought that little girl was something

special. She might take some of that sadness away."

"Oh Lord," she whispered. "I've never been the motherly type."

In a few minutes she added, "I'll tell you what, though. This would be a good place to raise a kid."

Ted found that she was just the right height, that he could bow his own head a little, and rest his cheek against her hair. It didn't seem like intruding.

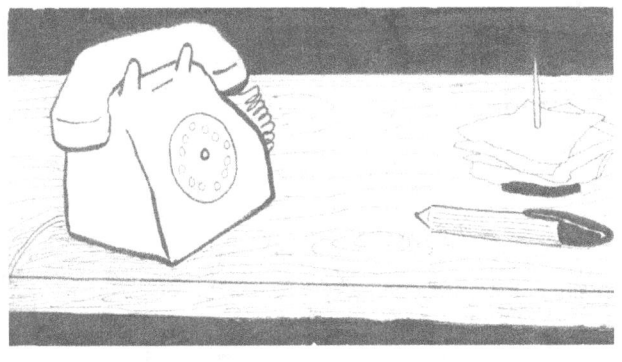

Uncle Gene

The minute I laid eyes on her, I said to myself, "Now there's a pretty woman."

For the class of '72, in my hometown of Redfern, any young woman who took to the style of "hippies," with long, loose dresses and matching hair, moved out. Those who stayed after graduating wore their hair short, some still in a beehive like their momma's. They wore jeans and cotton blouses for everyday. Most of them married soon and had children quick; some took jobs in the furniture factories, where they learned to smoke and make production. Their bodies went one of two ways, mostly: either they got wiry and thin, bent at the shoulder and the small of the back so they formed a tough little "s" with their spines, or they got round and lumpy like dumplings, with short hair in tight permanents that turned gray early and stayed that way. They were the church-goers, those round women, and on Sundays they wore bright-colored polyester double-knit pants and matching tops.

I hate polyester pants.

Since the accident, I haven't been able to see much more than outlines and suggestions, but with the light of the open door behind her, I could tell that this girl was neither too skinny nor too soft. She was tall, and held her shoulders back, so as not to deny that generous bosom. She wore a hippie-length dress made of some light fabric that lifted and floated in the little breeze in the doorway, and her hair fell around her shoulders; I thought it looked like it played in the breeze, too. Her hips, round and full like her breasts, were outlined against the daylight outside.

The ghost tips of my fingers, that had been gone for fourteen years, itched and burned with the sudden and unexpected desire to cradle those breasts and stroke those hips.

The first time I saw it, I thought the Alleghany Bar and Grill was a dark little cave, a place where old bears would go to den. I have never changed my mind about that. The first thing I really saw was the jukebox at the opposite side of the room, because it was lit up from inside. It glowed in the cigarette and cigar smoke like a lighthouse in a fogbank. Then I saw the humped backs of the old men at the counter, and the solid shadows that were the booths along the opposite wall. There was a man working behind the counter, and light coming through an opening behind him.

And there was Uncle Gene. He was sitting just as Brad had said he would be, at the one and only table, at the rear, beside the jukebox. He had on the derby hat, and he was smoking a cigarette in a holder that was five or six inches long, just as Brad had said he would be. There was a telephone on the table near his elbow, and a guitar leaning on the wall behind him. That was all I could see of him, at first.

Brad touched my back, and we moved forward together, wading into the smoke and darkness.

They came to my table like two little children tiptoeing through the dark forest. Like Hansel and Gretel. I guess that made me the wicked old witch.

"Hey, Uncle Gene," he said.

"Hello, Nephew." Brad was a good kid, if a little on the light side. Too much of his momma in him, I guess; she is the soft one, even though that man she married while she was

174

off at college, Brad's father, thought *he* was the artist. I guess that was why he never came around, the artistic side of him couldn't take the sight of me. Not that it kept him from being tough – or mean, which usually passes for tough – in other ways. "Have a seat."

He pulled out a chair and held onto it while she sat down, then he sat down, scooting his chair a little closer to her side – away from my side.

"Gene, this is my girlfriend, Maria."

I nodded in her direction. "Nice to meet you, Maria," I said. I did not stick out my hand, but Brad had probably warned her about that.

"Nice to meet you, too," she said. "Brad's talked about you a lot."

"I'll bet," I said.

She didn't miss a beat. "He says you were the best thing in his life when he growing up."

Well. It wouldn't take too much to have been the best thing in Brad's life, in those days. Momma off working. Daddy gone and everybody glad about it. All I had to do was not beat him, and I'd be better than that turd.

"And he says you play a mean blues guitar."

He did? "Not much." I knocked some ash from my cigarette into the ashtray beside the telephone. "Just a hobby."

She smiled. This close up, I saw it as a quick glimpse of light-colored teeth. I smelled her, even through all the smoke. Something spicy, not flowery or sweet.

She put her hand on the table, in my direction. "Of course, he told me about your accident, too."

He had. Of course.

He told me that Gene had been driving a fuel truck. He had been coming towards Redfern from the tank farm, so the truck's tank was full, making it difficult to control. He'd come around the curve going downhill –maybe going a little too fast, Brad said – and met a car coming towards him, and he'd swerved to avoid hitting it. The rig jackknifed and gasoline spilled across the highway and as the truck skidded on the asphalt, it sparked. The spark set the whole thing on fire. Gene walked out of it, completely engulfed in flames.

It was a miracle that he'd lived, and the pain must have been beyond description. Beyond, certainly, anything the doctors could control. "I was so sorry to hear about your suffering," I said. "I'm sorry that anyone would have to go through that, especially someone who was so good to a little boy like Brad."

I wanted to make a connection with this man, who had withstood so much and had found the strength in himself to love the child Brad had been. Brad said that once the doctors realized Gene was going to live, they did as much plastic surgery as the time and patient's condition allowed. They used skin from his back to cover most of his face. They took some from his upper arms to make some kind of lips for him. They gave up on his ears, and his hair never grew back – so Gene took to wearing that hat.

After that, Gene made them stop. Too much cost for too little gain, he'd said. People would just have to take him as he was.

The phone rang, and I automatically raised my right hand to pick up the receiver. Maria must've thought I was reaching for her, ready for a handshake or something. She took my right hand in both of hers.

I looked at her face. Even with my burnt-out eyes, I can tell. I can tell when people flinch, when they pull back, when they feel the scars or the funny, too-tight skin and they think, "Oh god, he's a monster," and they drop it like as if it was still hot, still on fire. You'd think my scars were burning them.

She didn't do it, though. She held on. I actually had time to feel her skin, which was cool and firm, and smooth.

176

No trauma, there. Nothing bad had ever happened to that hand, I thought. That hand had never caused anything bad to happen. She cradled my right hand in her left, and with her other hand she kind of stroked my wrist and the top of my hand, and her skin was cool and her fingertips gentle; they moved gently, gently, like she was smoothing away a spider web. She didn't even look at it. She looked at me.

These are the hands that tousled Brad's hair, I thought. These are the hands that showed him how to bait a hook, and tie his shoes, and comb his hair for church. Here is the man who had to use these poor, scarred hands to show Brad everything good.

The phone rang again, and I moved, slipping away from her to answer it. "This is Gene," I said. I was a little breathless. Some guy wanted to be picked up and delivered to the grocery store. I told him it would be four or five minutes, and hung up. Had to think a second to remember who was here, then said towards the last booth, six or eight feet away, "Buddy, pick up at 422 Center. Guy wants to buy groceries."

Buddy shuffled off of the bench seat, headed towards the back door. I got two late-models out there, "Gene's Taxi" on the doors. People call here, I send out one of the guys in one of the cars. It's not making anybody rich, but it keeps the bar tab down. It's something, something for me and the other losers to do.

"Would you like a drink?" I asked.

"I'll get them," Brad said, but she put her hand on his shoulder and said, "No, you stay here and talk to your uncle. I'll get the drinks. What for you, Uncle Gene?"

She didn't have to go to the bar. If I wave, Bill comes over. If it's just me, I don't even have to say it, he just brings the regular. But she was standing there, touching Brad, looking at me. "High Life on tap," I said, and she walked away. Not hesitating to go to the bar for a beer. My god.

"She's something, isn't she?" Brad said, and I turned my not-face towards him.

"Yeah."

"She's the one, Uncle Gene," he said, all quiet and serious.

"The one?" Sometimes it's a good thing nobody can read what I'm thinking. Or maybe, maybe if what I think or feel could be seen on my face, I'd go look in a mirror right now, and figure this one out.

"The one I want to marry."

"Have you asked her yet?"

"No."

God, young people are stupid. They don't know nothing. They don't know nothing about what they can lose and how fast it can disappear. "Then hurry up, man, a good woman like that won't lack for proposals."

He grinned at me, his grin that is just like his mother's. It reminded me, "Your mother know yet?"

"No, I wanted to talk it over with you first."

What next? What next? I couldn't take much more of this. Just then she got back to the table with three beers, put one in front of me, set down one for Brad, kept one for herself.

"Cheers," she said, raising up her glass, and Brad raised his. I wrapped what's left of both my hands around mine, raised it enough to be included, and stared hard at Brad. *Ask her*, I was trying to tell him. *Stake your claim, pronto.* And I guess I was trying to say thanks, too. *Thanks, man, for asking me, for wanting me to know.* Ain't that a laugh, old scarface trying to communicate.

He grinned. First at me, then at her. She smiled back, first at him, then at me. That flash of brightness.

There was something special about that time, those few minutes in the Alleghany Bar and Grill. Gene was such a good man, and we were so glad to be there with him. It meant so much to Brad.

After a little while they left. I was wore out with it all, with holding it all together. It's bad enough when nobody comes close, when all I have to do is sit and keep the pain at bay. Finally, after they were gone, I stood up, taking it slow. I got the little cane, tapped my way to the door, went out. My god, it was bright. I couldn't remember how long it had been since I was outside in the daylight. It hurts, you know. Heats up all the old scars, reminds me of everything. I have become a creature of the night, as they say. A real creep.

I walked to the curb, stopped and waited. When I heard something coming that I knew was a big pickup or farm truck, one that was building up speed to make it to the top of the hill before the light changed and the driver would have to stop and keep from rolling backwards while he waited for green, I stepped out. I knew my timing on this was good: the truck and I would meet head on, and I would get rid of the pain for good, and Brad and Maria would live without the old monster hanging around. They're good kids. They deserve a clean start.

A Little Larceny Among Friends

In 1985 a feeling that had been growing in my heart for years, that I had somehow missed out on all the good stuff, was in full bloom. I was the youngest in my family, and whenever the best family stories were brought out for airing and re-telling, I never had a role to remember. That's because they all took place in the hard times before Daddy got on with the state, before I was born. I had never had to wear somebody's hand-me-down boots with cardboard for insoles. I would never know what it was like to have to kill a chicken before Mama fried it. It was no big deal when I was accepted at Berea College, because three of my brothers and both of my sisters had already gone.

At Berea, it was clear that all the biggest battles to be fought in the War on Poverty had already been won: We were getting new roads all over the place, and coal mining was mostly seen as an automated business that, while it tore up the ground, could be a cash cow in terms of taxes and high wages. Everybody who wanted to belong to a union, did, and Highlands County's biggest political battles of the last ten years had been over whether the Ruitan Club should continue putting on the fiddlers' convention in the high school football field, or if they should move it to Dwight Barnes' big bottom field outside of town.

I had completely missed the major hippie action of which my older siblings had partaken. I wished desperately that I had been in on at least one march or sit-in. I agonized over the fact that the best music had happened before I could distinguish the Beatles from the Stones. By the time I left home, "illegal drugs" consisted primarily of marijuana and alcohol, and since most of the men who'd come home from Vietnam had brought with them a three-years' supply of pot seeds and also since running off a batch of corn liquor was the third largest source of income in Highlands County, there was no glamour in it for me. It was old hat. Common as cow shit.

About the only reactionary thing I could do was drop out of college and come home, so I did. I spent the next three years living with Mama and Daddy, letting my hair grow and waiting for an idea - any idea - to hit.

I was down at Kilby's General Store when an idea walked in on two legs. The legs were wrapped in size ten Lady Wrangler jeans, topped by a T-shirt with "STRANGE LOVE" printed at a strategic level. Above that came a head of black hair so full of curls and mystery that I would gladly have spent the next two years of my life exploring every little cave of it. Between the hair and the T-shirt was a pair of eyes the color of a rainbow trout, sometimes brownish and sometimes greenish and always full of glints and flickers of light. There must have been more of her, but these were the important parts. They're all I saw that day.

She walked down the aisle between the little snap-open cans of Beanie Weenies and Spaghettios and the bottles of mustard and ketchup, right up next to where all the old men were sitting. Conversation, which in that corner had not run high since the county agent had had an informational meeting about artificial insemination for better beef production, dried completely up. Some of the men pretended not to stare,

182

others plainly ogled. Delmer Watson stopped chewing. The cigarette between the three remaining fingers on Enoch Russell's left hand burned right down to the knuckle and 'Noch didn't even blink.

She knew what she was doing. She slowed down as she got near us, then stopped and looked us over. After about the amount of time it would have taken a heart to beat three or four times, if any of ours had been working, she smiled and said, "Hi."

Not one of us could speak.

She didn't seem surprised. "I'm looking for the bread," she said, slow and easy.

We all stared, witless as pigs. Finally Delmer poked one finger in the direction of the next aisle. "Over thar," he grunted.

She smiled again, directly at Delmer. "Thanks." As she went around the end of the cracker rack, every eye among the loafers strained against its cataract or adjusted for the point of correct focus in its bifocal lens. My own were locked on to that form as a man who was tumbling over the edge of a well would hang on to a rope.

She seemed to ignore us but stopped in front of the crackers, just where we could barely see her. She stood with her back to us for one moment, considering the saltines and the Ritzes. Finally she bent over from the waist and picked up a box of Zestas. And I realized that there was my idea. Every man in the loafing corner of Kilby's Store had the same idea, but I knew it was meant for me.

I stayed still as long as I could hear the murmur of her voice making back-up music to Wanda's bray. As soon as the screen door slapped shut behind my idea's departure, I hurried up to the check-out counter. I laid two apples beside the cash register, and a Milky Way, and a Pepsi.

"Say, who was that woman that was just in here?" I asked as I dug in my hip pocket for my wallet.

Wanda dropped the apples in a small bag, thereby

bruising them. She then bruised my spirit by giving me a smile more evil than usual. I used to date Wanda, but I'd gotten tired of her before she'd gotten tired of me. It didn't look like she'd ever get tired of making my life miserable in every little way she could manage.

"What woman, Norton?" Norton wasn't my real name. Somebody gave me that nickname when I was a kid, when I went through a stage of wearing a droopy vest and one of those cloth hats that were popular back in the early '70's. Some genius decided it made me look like Jackie Gleason's sidekick in that old television show, *The Honeymooners*, and it stuck. Wanda had quit calling me that when she and I were dating, but lately she had taken it up again, with a vengeance.

I watched as Wanda dropped my candy bar on top of the apples, and then dropped the Pepsi on top of the whole thing. More bruises for the apples, dents for the Milky Way. Without looking at her, I said, "I swear, Wanda, I pay good money for things in here, same as everybody else. I don't know why it has to be that I can't get a decent snack in exchange for it."

"Everything's got its price, Norton Blevins. Everything."

I picked up the bag and turned toward the door. "Do you know who that woman is, or don't you?"

"Oh yeah, I know. She's right good looking, if you like the type."

"And what type would that be?" I asked, though I knew better. I knew better than to ask Wanda for information about a pretty woman, and I knew better than to get into the gossip ring with Wanda. Her tongue was as sharp as her mind was dull, and there was almost nothing she liked better than using mean talk to beat up on people. Almost nothing.

"The Wolf Mountain type."

I waited. I knew Wanda wouldn't be able to keep her secret long - I think about 30 seconds is her record.

Sure enough, "That!" she said, and she smacked the

184

NO SALE button on the cash register to make the drawer slide out. She scooped a handful of coins from the side of the register and began sorting them into their little sections in the drawer. When as much time as she could stand had gone by, she continued, "Was Norma Baugess, Pres's niece that's come down to live with him. Probably intends to snag herself a husband and a daddy for that kid of hers."

Pres Baugess was a scion of the Wolf Mountain Baugesses, known for generations as the most independent and backwardest-living people in Highlands County. The family home was located in the upper end of a holler where the feet of two ridges were so close together that the house had its backside up against one mountain's ankle bone and its front porch against the other.

Woodrow, nicknamed President, shortened to Pres, was born in 1940, following a labor that lasted so long his mother finally agreed to be laid in the back of the '32 Ford truck the family kept parked at the big bend in the creek, and taken to the Greer Clinic in the county seat. Old Doc Greer had to do some cutting and pulling before he could get the baby out. It was blue and limp, but Doc worked on it for a few minutes, and then it pinked up and cried. Doc told them not to have too many expectations for the baby, because he had been without oxygen for who knew how long, with the cord twisted around his neck and him laying crosswise to the birth canal.

The boys carried the infant Woodrow and his mother back up Gravely Creek, where they both continued in tolerable good health. By the time he was 40 years old, Pres had an old man's appearance and a quirked kind of intelligence. He was soft and pale-looking, with colorless hair and faded blue eyes. He was picky about his clothes and always dressed the same, in polyester pants and dress shirts, with a narrow-brimmed straw hat on his head and a jacket folded over his right arm.

People said he didn't have the smarts to come in out

185

of the rain, but he was plenty sharp about trading, which was how he made his living. Pres always had something to trade or sell, a pocketknife or a bunch of oversized fingernail clippers with pictures of the Washington Monument on the handles, and he always had a roll of money in his pocket.

He would stroll into the store, ease into a group of men, ask about everybody's family, and pull out some trinket from his pocket. "I got an awful good bargain on these clippers," he might say, and before you knew it, eight people would've paid him a dollar each for a pair of fingernail clippers that they didn't need.

He dealt in bigger things than nail clippers, too, and if anybody in the county was in need of a particular item, they could go to Pres and make a request, and sooner or later, Pres would have one to sell. Anything. But Pres was particularly interested in guns. He continually bought, sold and traded for guns. He corresponded (dictating letters for someone else to write down, since he hadn't ever really gotten the hang of writing, as he freely admitted) about guns with people all across the United States, and even in foreign countries. The UPS man made a regular once-a-week stop at Pres's house, to pick up and deliver guns. And Pres kept a collection of long guns - rifles and shotguns - that people said was a sight to behold.

It was also true, as I had reason to know, that Pres sold a little pot on the side.

Despite his problematic beginnings and subsequent peculiarities, Pres had done well enough in his trading to buy a little piece of land down off the mountain, right in the community, and to have a four-room brick house built on it. He got around by hitching rides and walking, and he was an everyday sight, trudging along the shoulder of the road with his jacket over his arm, looking down with a thoughtful expression.

I went out the door of the store that day and got into

the '69 Chevy pickup Daddy had given to me to use. Instead of turning down the road toward home, I turned up, and sure enough, within a quarter of a mile I saw those Wranglers rolling smoothly up the side of the road. I passed her, then pulled across and stopped on the shoulder. She kept coming, and when she got nearly even with the driver's door, I opened it and leaned out. "Would you like a ride?" I asked.

She paused and seemed to consider, and then she smiled and took a deep breath, which caused the lettering on her T-shirt to expand. She tilted her chin up and said, "Yeah, I reckon I would."

I stood in front of the door while she got in the truck and slid across the seat. She passed so close to me I could smell her hair, a heavy musk and herb scent that made me want to bury my face in it. I crawled back in after her, and ground the gears trying to put the truck in first. In a few seconds I remembered to release the emergency brake.

"My name's Norma Baugess," she said.

"I know."

We covered nearly a mile before she said, "Well, I don't know your name."

"Oh! Nor- James. James Blevins."

"What did you start to say?" She hadn't buckled her seat belt, and now she turned sideways, resting her back against the passenger side door, her left leg up on the seat.

"Nothing."

She looked at me hard. I could feel her gaze. It made my skin prickle like a cool breeze on a sunburn. "I hate secrets," she said.

My face got hotter. "It's no secret. It's just a nickname."

I stopped, but she just sat there, looking at me.

"Norton. Everybody around here calls me Norton, after an old television show."

"Would you rather be called James?" she asked.

"Jim." Nobody had ever called me "Jim."

"Okay then, I'll call you Jim." She turned back to the front, for which I was both grateful and sad, and which made a difference (for the better) in my driving. When we got close to Pres's little brick house, she pointed and said, "Turn in right there."

"I know."

"You do? Word sure gets around fast, doesn't it?"

"Yeah, particularly when people are interested."

I pulled into the driveway and stopped near the front porch.

"Are you interested, Jim?"

I took one hand off the wheel and laid it along the back of the seat. "Oh yeah," I said.

She smiled at me and the light glinted in those eyes. "Well, that's good," she said, and popped open her door. "I'll see you, Norton-James-Jim." She slammed the door and crossed in front of the truck, then up the three steps onto Pres's front porch, then through the storm door into the dark indoors. I watched every inch of the way.

What Norma Baugess wanted was to get out of Highlands County. This was first impressed upon me a couple of weeks later, while I was deeply engrossed in an exploration of Norma's hair. I had set out on this journey of discovery by first pressing my face against the crown of her head, taking deep breaths of the scent of her hair and feeling its fine, lively texture against my cheek, with my lips, against my eyelids. I had followed the curve of her skull down to her ear - which I decided deserved a course of study of its own and which I promised myself I'd get back to - then to the point of her jaw, and was well on my way around her neck, touching, tasting and smelling every square quarter-inch of that incredible terra incognita, when Norma's voice, whispery and tender as a result (I thought) of my dutiful attention to the details of scrutiny and analysis, said, "Don't you want to get out of here, Jim?"

It took a few seconds to register. "Do I want to get out of here?" I said, and didn't care that I sounded even to myself like a kid who's been offered cotton candy at a fair. I pulled back slightly from Norma, and bumped my elbow against the steering wheel. "We could go to my brother Chester's house. Him and Judy are gone on vacation and I'm supposed to feed their dogs -"

"No, I don't mean out of *here*." She sat up and crossed her arms over her chest. "I mean out of this whole place. Highlands County. Don't you want to go to some real place, where every soul you meet doesn't already know your family story for six generations and have you pegged, right down to the kind of pop you drink?"

"It don't make a lick to me who knows I always drink Pepsis." I leaned forward so I could explore the other side of Norma's neck and the dark waves of hair that curled over it. "What do you think about Judy's house?"

She turned her face a little, giving me better access to the back of her neck. "Judy's house," she whispered, "is not nearly far enough away."

After that, the idea of going away kept cropping up in conversations between me and Norma. Which is not to say she harped on it, but the subject did seem to arise whenever I was most deeply involved in mapping delightful new parts of Norma's anatomy. Finally, I got the idea of leaving Highlands County sort of tangled up with the idea of necking, and the mention or prospect of one just naturally carried with it the hope of the other. If Norma said something like, "Maybe we could go to Myrtle Beach, and you could get a job building houses. You know how to build things, don't you Jim?" I'd pull her into my arms and start kissing whatever part of her came closest, quickest. It got to where actually considering living in some other place was enough to make me light-headed. Some relief was going to have to be had, one way or the other, or I was going to blow a fuse.

The trouble was money. I didn't have any, and Norma didn't either. Even in my fogged condition I knew that if she'd had enough cash to buy a bus ticket to anywhere, Norma would be at least tempted to walk out the door and be gone. A few things held her back. I pretended to myself that I was one of them, but in my heart I knew better. But there was no way she'd leave her little girl, or put herself in the position of not knowing where the kid's next meal or warm bed was coming from. Angel was a year-and-a-half old, and everybody said she was a living doll. She had dark curly hair like her mother, and big round blue eyes. The one time I asked about Angel's father, Norma slid out of my arms and looked me hard in the face and told me that Angel's father did not exist in this world and if I wanted to continue my relationship with Norma that would be the last word I'd ever say about him.

I had no problem with that.

But Norma couldn't get a job because she couldn't leave Angel with a baby-sitter. "Nobody'd take care of her the way I do," she said, and she was probably right. The only time she left Angel so we could go out was after Angel was asleep, and Pres was there to watch her. She'd remind Pres of every-thing he had to do if Angel coughed or rolled over or - God forbid - woke up, and she'd tell Pres about fifty times that we'd be back in TWO HOURS. And you'd better believe that we'd be back in two hours. No jealous daddy with a shotgun behind the door ever demanded and received such absolute obedience as Angel got from her momma.

I was doing pick-up work, cutting and selling loads of stove wood or working in somebody's Christmas trees for a few days at a time. I did odd jobs, mowing, maybe painting a barn roof. I stayed busy but I never could get any money ahead.

Norma said we had to have enough money to get to some "decent" place and get settled and to tide us over un-til I got a job and could pay the bills. (My fingertips tingled as they wandered among the gentle little hills and valleys of

Norma's spine.) She had it all figured out. She said we'd need three thousand dollars.

"Three thousand dollars!" I straightened up so fast I nearly whiplashed my neck. "Three *thousand* ? What'll we need three thousand dollars for? Are we going to live in a high-rise hotel and eat caviar three times a day?"

Norma let her fingers do a little exploring of their own, along my jaw and down around the top button of my shirt. "Stuff adds up," she said, her voice sort of low and lazy. "Deposit on rent and utilities, a few pieces of furniture, traveling expenses. We'd have to have enough to tide us over until you started getting regular paychecks."

I thought about undoing that button, to let her fingers cover more territory. I bent nearer, and my voice was lower, too. "And what else?" I said.

"Three thousand would keep us comfortable until we got settled in. Jim." Her voice dropped to a whisper as she repeated my name, "Jim. Wouldn't it be great to be away from here?"

I tightened my arms around her and pulled her closer. I would've liked to have absorbed her right into my body.

That was sort of a high point, and after that things started going down hill. There was no way I was ever, ever in this world, going to save three thousand dollars from doing odd jobs. When I tried to impress this upon Norma, she first suggested I get a "real" job, and when I gave her the cold, hard facts about the 9.7 percent unemployment rate in Highlands County and reminded her that I was just a first-year-of-college drop-out with no real job experience, she looked at me long and hard.

"James Blevins," she said, "I am not staying in Highlands County forever. If you want to be with me when I leave, you'd better think of a way to get some money."

"But how?" I was in torment, with all this talk about leaving coupled with the idea of me not going. "Nobody in my family has that kind of money setting around, waiting to be used. Hell, nobody in Highlands County has that kind of money!"

"Oh yes they do," she said.

"Who? You just name me one person who could cough up three thousand dollars without putting his granddaddy's farm in hock. Just one!"

She looked at me as cool as shade in October, and said, "Well, Uncle Pres, for one. He has money stashed all over the house."

My jaw dropped and I stood in front of Norma and for once, for probably the first time since I'd watched her buying crackers in Kilby's Store, I tried to not notice how she looked. I tried to think about what she'd just said.

"You think Pres Baugess has three thousand dollars in cash laying around in his house?" I finally managed to say.

"I think he's got more. Lots more."

I hated to say the next thing. I had a sneaking suspicion that if it wasn't for me coming up with the money she thought was necessary for her great escape, Norma wouldn't have been giving me the time of day, much less an invitation to accompany her on the trip. But in simple honesty I had to point out to her, "Why don't you just ask Pres if he'd loan it to you?"

She jerked her head a little and looked away. "I did. He wouldn't do it."

I didn't say anything, and she went on, "I sort of overplayed my hand with Pres. The family always talks about how much money he's got, I'd heard about it all my life. When I came down off the mountain and asked to stay with him, I was planning to ask him for a loan. But I figured I ought to wait a little while, so he could get to know me and Angel, and start thinking of us as sort of like his family, you know? So he'd be more likely to loan us the money?"

I nodded.

"But he likes us too much."

192

"Too much?"

"I asked him, but he won't give me any money because he don't want us to leave. He says he'll buy me or Angel anything we want. Specially Angel, he'd give that child a star out of the sky, if she wanted it and he could get it. But he won't give me any cash. He thinks of us as his family now, all right enough. He wants us to stay with him forever and ever."

Norma clenched her hands into fists and crossed her arms across her chest, packing the fists up under her arms. "I'd steal that money myself, but I can't. I can't. I can't steal from my own family."

Too much information was coming at me too fast. I couldn't keep up with it. I had just barely worked my way through the notion that Pres liked Norma and Angel so much he wouldn't let them leave. Only one word of Norma's last statement got through to me. "Steal?" I said.

Now Norma turned towards me and stepped a little closer. Her hands were still up under her arms. "It would be more like a loan, really. We could pay him back when we got set up. And it's not like Pres needs the money. He never spends any money, he just keeps trading and selling stuff and turning profits and never spending anything. He's got money stuck in jars in the kitchen and under the couch cushions and everywhere. He might not even miss it."

"If it's a loan, you take it out."

"No, I can't." She turned away again and started to pace. She stopped near the window and put her forehead against the glass, and for a moment I imagined myself as that glass, cool under her skin. "Jim, Pres really loves us. He treats me better than anybody ever has. And Angel, Angel would as soon sit in his lap as in mine." Her voice dropped to a whisper. "But I have got to get her out of here. If I don't take Angel out, she'll grow up knowing she's one of the Wolf Mountain Baugesses. She'll think a certain way because that's the way people expect her to think. She won't be able to see any roads but the ones that just go in circles, round and round Highlands County. She's got to know better." She had her eyes squeezed shut, but I could see tears sliding out from under the lids, making shiny trails down her cheeks.

I walked over and put my arms around her. I pressed my cheek against her head and said, "Okay Norma, okay now. We'll get the money. I promise I'll get the money to take you and Angel away. Uncle Pres won't even know it's gone." She turned inside my arms until her face was against my chest, and she boo-hooed until I thought I couldn't stand another second of it. Then she calmed down and started making plans.

Norma hunted out all the little stashes of money in Pres's house. She made a list, like: under couch cushion, $200; peanutbutter jar in cabinet, right side of sink, $87 (all ones); left boot in back of closet, $450; sugar bowl on back of stove, $52; old sock in underwear drawer, $320.

"My god, Norma, did you have to go poking around in Pres's underwear?"

"People always hide stuff in their underwear drawers. Besides, Pres never gets in that drawer. He must wear the same shorts for weeks, maybe till they just fall off."

My stomach was a little troubled by that image.

"It don't add up," she said.

"What don't?" I was still trying not to think about Pres's underwear.

"The money! I know Pres makes gobs of money. Last week I saw him trade a guy two old guns for one other old gun, and after the guy left, Pres told me the one he kept was one of only two like it in the world. In the *world*, Jim. He said it was worth over ten thousand dollars, and - " A funny look came over Norma's face, and she stopped talking.

"And what?" Tell me something, I thought, tell me anything to take the place of the picture of old Pres walking down the road, and shreds of stained and rotted boxers coming sliding out of his pants leg. I could just see him, standing

194

on one foot while he shook the other one, to rid himself of the last bits of -

"And then he just stuck that ten thousand dollar gun under the couch."

"He did what?" Pres was, mercifully, banished from my mind.

Norma got down on her knees and reached under the couch. She fumbled around for a few seconds, and then she dragged out a big, heavy-looking rifle, with several dust bunnies attached. She frowned, lifted up the skirt of the couch, and pressed her cheek against the floor so she could look under there. Then she used the rifle to rake out a little tin box that fancy crackers had come in. It had dust bunnies too.

The box clanked, and Norma had to use some muscle to lift it up onto her lap. She popped the lid off, and I scooted over so I could see what was in there. It was coins, stacked in piles and the piles held together with rubber bands.

"Looks like fifty-cent pieces," I said, and leaned over to get a better look.

"No, not fifty-centses. Dollars. Uncle Pres used to give all the kids a silver dollar at Christmas, 'til there was so many of us he couldn't afford it any more. Then he switched off to Kennedy half-dollars. But these are silver dollars. Look at the date on this one. 1894."

"Hey, that could be worth something!" I said, and reached for the box, but Norma pushed my hand away.

"We're not going to mess with these."

"We're not? But why not? Look, Norma, there's one, two, three, four, five, six stacks in a row; four rows across; there must be what, ten or twelve in a stack? That's something like... I don't know, is that 240 silver dollars? And if they were only worth ten dollars each, that's two thousand and four hundred dollars, right?"

"It don't matter. These are not for us." Norma put the lid back on the box and bent over to shove it under the couch, but I grabbed her arm and held it.

"But why, Norma? These are ready cash! I thought you were so hot to get out of Dodge." I really wanted to handle those coins, to let them spill through my fingers and listen to their clink as they fell against each other. But Norma's jaw was set at a stubborn angle, and the corners of her mouth were turned down like she might be about to cry.

"Because," was all she said.

"Norma, you're not making any sense."

"I don't care whether I'm making sense or not. We're not taking the silver dollars."

She shoved the box back under the couch and then picked up the gun. It didn't look to me like it was worth ten thousand dollars. It was a bolt-action, its stock made out of some dark wood, its metal parts dark too. It looked a lot like Dad's old .30-06, that I used to shoot groundhogs, except it wasn't all banged up. I looked at it in Norma's hands, resting across her thighs as she sat there on the floor of Pres's living room, and sighed. Then I reached over and picked it up.

"Are you sure this is it?" I asked.

Norma nodded, and just then we heard Angel stirring around on the bed she and Norma shared, waking up from her nap. Norma whispered, "Take it out of here," and stood up. I looked at the gun in my hand for a few seconds, then got up too. I went out and opened the pickup door, and then stood there wondering where, in such a small area as a pickup, I could hide a gun. Finally I dragged out a couple of cloth sacks that chicken feed had come in, and wrapped the gun in them. I used the gun to punch down the pop cans and candy wrappers and junk that was piled behind the seat, and then laid the wrapped gun on top. I tossed a couple of things that had been rolling around in the floor on top for good measure, and stood back to look. It appeared pretty much like the junk in 98 percent of all the pickups in Highlands County. I started to the house, then stopped and looked back. Something I'd read in a story for some high school English class tried to make itself heard inside my head. I went back to the truck,

196

pulled the gun out of all the trash, unwrapped it, hung it in the rack behind the pickup seat. That story had been about hiding things in plain view. If 98 per cent of pickups had trash behind the seat, about 110 percent had rifles hanging in the back windows.

I slammed the door, satisfied with my cleverness, but when I turned around, there was Pres, coming across the yard straight for me. My bowels clenched, and I just knew he'd seen me hanging his gun in my pickup.

Pres came on in his usual posture, right arm bent at the elbow so that his hand rested against his stomach, tan jacket folded neatly over his arm, hat set square on his head. He strolled right up to me and said, "Good evening, James. You've come to see Norma, I guess."

"Yeah," I said, though my voice came out sort of shaky.

"Well, let's go in and see if she's to home." He turned and walked toward the porch, and I followed. When we went in, Norma was sitting on the couch. Angel was sitting in her lap, eating slices of apple that Norma had cut up into a bowl.

"There's my girls," Pres said, and I realized that, usually, Pres Baugess didn't let much emotion come through his voice. I'd never thought about it before, but Pres always sounded the same, whether he was telling you about a set of steak knives he had to sell, or that somebody had died. I realized it now because there was pleasure in his voice when he talked about "his girls," and it sounded so different. Anybody would've noticed.

Angel looked up and smiled a great big smile that reminded me who her mother was. She held out a piece of apple to Pres, and he walked right over and took it out of her sticky little fist. Then he sat down next to Norma and Angel and put the apple in his mouth. He didn't make a big production out of it, like some adults would have, trying to suck up to a little kid. He just put it in his mouth and chewed and said, in his usual calm, flat tone, "I believe that's about the best apple I ever tasted."

Angel had not taken her eyes off Pres's face, from the minute he walked in the door until he said that about the apple. Then she smiled at her momma and crawled out of Norma's lap and into Pres's. They set there on the couch, sharing the apple. I looked at Norma, and she had this awful expression on her face, like a mixture of fear and sorrow, like she was looking at the face of somebody she used to love but who had changed into something evil. Pres appeared the same as always, to me, and I knew that look wasn't for her little Angel, so I didn't know what she was thinking about.

I set down in the big, lumpy chair that matched the couch, and waited for something to happen. Pres and Angel ate apple until the bowl was empty, and then Pres said, "Well, I asked Roger Steele to stop by on his way home, to help me write a letter to a man about a gun. If I'd knowed you'd be here, James, I wouldn't-a asked him. You could've done it for me, I reckon."

I fairly leaped out of that chair. "I gotta go. I've got some things I got to do. I promised Mom I'd bring home a loaf of bread. She'll be wanting it before supper, and I guess I'd better go. I'll see you later, Norma. Bye!" I tried not to run as I hurried to the door. Roger is a county deputy, the middle son of the Steeles from over on Blackstone Creek, and as fine a local police officer as Highlands County has ever seen. He is pretty smart, and has spent the ten years of his law enforcement career proving to everybody that he won't play favorites when it comes to diligently chasing down perpetrators, even if they are members of his home community, not even if they happened to be the younger brother of his best buddy and fishing partner. As I happened to be. Roger Steele was a good man, and the last person on this earth I wanted to see right then.

I slammed the storm door open, and was ready to jump off the edge of the porch nearest to the driveway when Roger's cruiser turned in. I froze while it gently pulled up behind my truck and Roger shut the engine off.

He opened the door and sat with one foot on the ground while he spoke into the two-way radio. Then he stepped out, adjusted his belt (which made the leather holster creak and the handcuffs jingle) and strolled over to the porch. "Hey, Norton," he said, "How's it hanging?"

"Ah, pretty good, I guess," I said, but I sounded weak.

"Been seeing your truck parked here a lot, lately. You and Miss Norma Ann an item now, or are you going into business with Pres?"

"Yeah, business with Pres." I tried to laugh a little. "I wouldn't be any help to Pres, I don't know a thing about guns. Just nothing. Wouldn't know if one was worth anything special, if it was handed to me. Pretty much all look alike to me. Never was much interested in guns." If my mouth kept on running like that, I was going to have to slap both hands over it. Different parts of my body seemed out of control: my mouth wouldn't accept an order to shut down, my knees were knocking on their own volition, and I was having to think hard to keep from dirtying my pants. I always did have problems with my digestive system.

Roger looked at me for a minute while he was apparently working something left over from lunch out of his back teeth. Finally he said, "Can you stick around for a few minutes, Norton? There's something I need to talk over with you."

"Sure, sure, I can wait. No problem."

"I need to do a little letter-writing for Pres." Roger climbed the steps onto the porch and walked through the doorway. I had whacked the storm door so hard it hadn't even closed behind me. I heard Roger's voice greeting Norma and Pres, and then he was talking to Angel. Angel is not a big talker, but Roger has four kids of his own, and he got her to say a word or two. Then Norma came out onto the porch, carrying Angel.

She came up close to me and whispered, "Let's get out of here."

"Can't," I whispered back. "He wants to tell me something. Besides, I can't get my truck out 'til he moves his car." I pointed to the driveway.

"What does he want to tell you?"

"How am I supposed to know? He hasn't told me, yet."

"Are you in any trouble?"

"Trouble? No, I am not in any trouble! Or at least, I wasn't, until you got me into it."

"Listen, James Blevins, I did not get you into anything you didn't want to get into. I am not going to take the blame for this. My daughter needs me, and I can't be leaving her to go off and serve jail time or whatever. I am not the one who took the gun and has it hidden at this very moment in his truck."

"Blame? Who said anything about blame? But when you come right down to it, it wasn't my idea to -" Norma and I had been whispering to each other like a pair of snakes arguing over a frog dinner, but suddenly Roger's voice cut through.

"Hey Norton!" he yelled. "Can you come here a minute?"

I stared into Norma's eyes, those beautiful shimmery-trout eyes, and after a few seconds I called back, "Sure, Roger. Coming."

Pres and Roger were in the kitchen, sitting at the table. There was a tablet of lined paper in front of Roger, and an ink pen, and he was holding a big pistol in his hands. Pres was sitting across from him, looking exactly the same way he always looked, unruffled and mild.

"Come here, Norton. I may need a witness." I walked over and stood at Roger's elbow. "Now Pres," Roger says, serious but steady, "everybody here needs to understand a few things. You invited me in to your house, didn't you?"

"Yes," Pres replied. Straight and simple. I admired that.

"And you brought this gun out to show me, didn't you?"

Roger held the pistol out towards Pres.

"Yes."

"Pres, haven't I talked to you before about needing to have a license to buy and sell weapons? And about having to list the guns' serial numbers, and have a copy of the list with the sheriff?"

"Oh yes, Roger, I remember. I understand all that. You came and made a list, and you carried it to the sheriff for me. Everything was done all clear and legal." Pres didn't sound worried at all.

"Well then, Pres, how come I didn't know about this gun? How come it doesn't have a serial number engraved on it anywhere? Do you have a receipt for this gun?" Roger was talking a little softer now, but still real calm. Real steady.

"Oh. I just got this gun. I traded Andrew Hamm, from over on the Wilburn Mountain Gap, two luger pistols for this gun. He served in the War, you know, and wanted some of them German pistols like the enemy used to have."

Roger sighed and laid the pistol on the table. He rubbed his face with one hand. "Pres, you've got to get a receipt every time. Trade or buy or sell, get them to sign a paper."

"I know," Pres said, "but Andrew Hamm can't write either." And he left it at that.

"Ah Lord," Roger muttered under his breath. "Pres, do you have any more guns on the premises that aren't registered?"

"Well, I believe there might be another one or two." Pres looked at the ceiling for a minute and then added, "James, there's a little old box under my bed, would you go get it and bring it in here?"

Without saying anything I went into Pres's bedroom, the back bedroom. It was stuffy in there. There was one window, but it was covered by curtains pulled together. There was a double bed with blankets that looked like they had been slept on top of. There was a big gun cabinet with a lot of rifles packed in it. I got down on my knees and lifted up the quilts and blankets hanging down from the top of the bed, and looked, but I couldn't see a thing under there. It was dark as pitch. I laid flat on my stomach and reached with my arm as far as I could, and patted my hand around. At first all I could feel was little hard things like dried bug bodies, and lots of soft, fluffy stuff that was probably the dust of untold generations. But then I scooted up near the head of the bed and my fingers ran into the edge of a cardboard box, and I pulled it out. It was about 20 inches square, and heavy.

I carried it into the kitchen and set it on the table.

"Would you like to open it up and show me what you've got in there?" Roger had his head propped up on his left hand, and a tone in his voice that meant he didn't really want to see what was in that box, but knew he was going to anyway.

Pres didn't speak, but pulled up the flaps of the box, and started pulling out pistols and laying them on the table in a row. There were twelve of them.

"That's a lot of pistols," Roger said, without lifting his jaw from his hand.

"Pistols is popular right now," Pres said in that calm, almost prissy way he has. "Now right here is one that I could let you have for a bargain. I traded for it from a man over in the coal fields. He said it'ud been in his family for four generations, but he needed some money awful bad, and I give it to him. This is a Civil War officer's pistol, but it's from the Union side. I don't know how his great-granddaddy come to have it, unless he was a-fightin' for the Union, or else he might'uv took it off a dead Yankee. Lots of soldiers did, you know."

Roger reached out and took the pistol, and brought it back close to his face to see it better. After a few seconds he laid it gently on the table and said, "My god, Pres, how do you come by such things?"

"There was a man over in the coal fields, and - "

"No, never mind, I know how you got this gun, I just

202

mean... never mind. Do you have papers for this gun?"

"Don't believe I do."

"Do you have papers for any of these?"

Pres looked at the row of pistols, laying hard and black, unalterable as sin on the shiny table top. "Well now, *this* one right here, I believe I've had this one for quite a while. It might have been on that list you made and took to the sheriff. Does this one look familiar to you?" He picked up one of the smaller pistols and held it out to Roger.

Roger sighed and without looking at Pres he said, "Are there any other guns in this house for which you do not have the proper receipts and registrations?"

Pres looked off into the distance, and then said, "James, there's a .300 Magnum in my bedroom closet, and a .270 Winchester in the cabinet there under the sink." He brought his eyes back to Roger's face and said in that same placid way, "I reckon this means I'm in trouble with the law?"

"Pres, you might be in all kinds of trouble. Norton, bring me those guns."

I had had time to settle down a little, and realized I was probably not in any immediate danger. I ought to have been feeling a little sorry for old Pres, maybe, but all I could think about was that *ten thousand dollar gun* hanging behind the seat in my pickup, and thank you God, thank you God, just let Roger get on with persecuting poor old Pres and if you let me get out of this I promise I'll put that gun back under the couch and never consider stealing again. Never. Never even be tempted, I swear.

Meantime, Pres had me running all over the house, hauling guns out from under furniture and from behind doors. (He didn't even suggest I open the gun cabinet in his room or the one in Norma's room, which were packed full of what must have been legitimate, signed for and listed weapons.) When he got done, there were eight long guns laying on the table with the twelve pistols. Roger had put his hands over his eyes after about the third or fourth rifle, and from behind his hands he finally said, "Tell me that's all of them, Pres. Please."

Pres gazed upward again, and whispered to himself for a minute, and then turned to Roger. "Well, there's one more. I almost forgot it because I've only had it a day. Go look under the couch, James. There's a special one under there."

My feet were stuck to the floor.

Roger took his hands away from his eyes and looked at the arsenal on the table. He sighed. "Pres, what am I going to do with you? You know better than to deal in weapons without the proper paperwork."

Pres just sat there with his mouth set in its usual half-smile.

Roger sighed again. He seemed very glum. "Maybe we can make a list and describe the circumstances of how you came into possession of each of these weapons, and go from there." He brought his eyebrows down and leaned forward a little. "Maybe," he put a lot of emphasis on that word, "the sheriff won't put you into jail for longer'n about ten years, for this."

I noticed that Pres's eyes widened a little, but I was beyond being aware of much else.

Roger glanced at me and said, "Go get that other gun, Norton. Let's get this over with."

I pulled my boot up off the floor, and took a step that felt the way those guys who fooled around on the surface of the moon looked, or like Frankenstein in the old movies. I was stiff. It took the effort of my whole body to lift one leg and then the other. I knew I was moving like a dead man, like a guilty man. I would've arrested me on the strength of that walk alone, if I'd been a policeman. And though I couldn't feel it, I knew my face was corroborating evidence. All Roger had to do was look.

Thank goodness he was too busy looking somewhere else.

I staggered into the living room and stood in the middle of the floor, staring at the couch. Norma had been playing with Angel on their bed, and now she came to my side. "What's going on?" she mouthed at me.

I just looked at her, my mouth halfway open and my eyes opened all the way.

"Jim?" she whispered, and shook my elbow a little.

"James?" came Pres's voice. "Just look under the couch there. It's right there."

Now Norma's eyes opened up. Her shoulders sort of hunched a little, too.

Still moving like a marionette, I dropped to my knees and laid my cheek against the floor. I closed my eyes and if wishing could ever make things happen, that gun would've transmigrated from my pickup to under that couch in that instant. I opened my eyes, and stuck my arm under there. Nothing. I swept my hand back and forth, just like I didn't know that gun was somewhere else.

"James?" I swear, Pres's voice hadn't changed one iota, the whole afternoon. He might have been inquiring about the weather.

"Norton!" Roger's chair creaked, like he was leaning back in it. "Bring it on in here, boy."

"There's no gun under the couch," I croaked.

I thought I heard Roger mutter, "Thank you, Jesus." In a few seconds Pres came into the room, and Roger was right behind him. Pres got down on his knees and bent over so that his butt was higher than any other part of him. He stuck his arm under the couch and felt around. He grunted a little, and crawled around in a circle so he could stick his other arm under there, and he felt around some more. Then he looked up and said, "Why, where's my ten thousand dollar gun?"

Norma and I stood like we had been struck into pillars of salt, as still as Lot's wife who had been caught looking into the site of sin, too. I couldn't even move the muscles necessary to roll my eyes enough to see Norma's beautiful face. Roger stuck his head forward a little and said, "Did you say... *ten thousand dollar gun?*"

"One of only two like it in the world." Pres's voice now had a little emotion. It sounded surprised. "I got it from a man just yesterday. I heard about this man down in South Carolina a-having this gun, and I wrote and inquired about it, and we struck a deal. The man's nephew carried him up here just yesterday. I put the gun right here."

"You put a gun worth ten thousand dollars under your couch?" Roger's voice was surprised, too. "Are you sure?"

"Oh yes. I put it right *here.*"

"Well, let's look around. It might be somewhere in the house." When Roger turned to start searching, he bumped into Norma. He put his hands out and held her shoulders, to steady her and to sort of set her aside. As he did, while his eyes were already looking around the room for any extra guns that might be just laying there, he said, "Norma, did you see this fancy gun Pres is talking about?" Without waiting for an answer he stepped to the big chair, pulled it out from the wall and looked behind it, then pulled the cushion off the seat and looked there.

Norma swallowed hard and said, "I was here when those men came. Two men, one old, one real young. They carried a gun in, but then I took Angel into the bedroom, to let them do their business in private. I don't know anything that happened after that."

Roger was still searching the living room, looking under and behind everything. "It was a long gun, a rifle, wasn't it, Pres? Norma, why don't you go look all over in your room, and Norton, check out the kitchen. Pres, let's me and you go through your room."

Pres put his hands on the couch to help him lever up from the floor. "I declare, Roger, I'm mighty shook up. Do you mind if I smoke a joint before we start in my room, to steady my nerves?"

206

I had been hurrying off to the kitchen, glad to get a little space between me and Roger's uniform, but when I heard Pres say that, my foot stopped in mid-air and my jaw dropped and I whipped my head around, turning to make sure I'd heard what I thought I'd heard. Roger was staring at Pres.

"What?" was all he said.

Pres was moving my way. I realized he was on his way to the kitchen, where he kept a pound or two of good-quality pot in the vegetable crisper in his refrigerator. As I had reason to know.

"I need a joint."

"Of *pot*?" Roger's voice had gone from surprise to shock.

"It's awful good for your nerves," Pres said as he opened the 'frige door.

Roger just stood there and watched while Pres got a paper from the packet on top of the 'frige, filled it with marijuana from the vegetable crisper, and carefully rolled it up. Then Pres went to the window behind the sink, where a box of strikes-anywhere matches was laying on the windowsill, and lit his joint. He took a good big hit, and Roger stepped into the kitchen and said,

"Woodrow Baugess, I am placing you under arrest for possession and use of a controlled substance, and possession with intent to distribute." He went over and took the joint out of Pres's hands and extinguished it by holding the end of it under the faucet and running water over it. Then he laid the joint carefully on the edge of the sink and got his handcuffs off the back of his belt. "Swear to God, Pres, I ought to arrest you for plain, blinding stupidity. You have the right to remain silent, you have the right to an attorney before questioning. Questioning? Hell, I don't have to question a thing except why you thought you could break the law right in front of my eyes, right under my nose. Pres, what in the world is wrong with you?"

"You mean it's against the law to smoke a joint in my own house?"

"Lord, help." Roger bent his head and I believe that, there for a second, he was praying. Maybe for Pres to wise up, or else for the burden of Pres's stupidity to be lifted from his, Roger's, shoulders. Then he (gently, I noticed) pulled Pres's arms behind him and snapped the 'cuffs on. "Sit down here, Pres," he said, and steered him to the kitchen chair he'd been setting in before. "I've got to go out to the cruiser and call for help."

"What about my gun?" Pres asked. He leaned toward Roger just a little and said, like as if they were sitting down at the office and Roger hadn't just put handcuffs on him, "You know, I believe I've been robbed."

"The way my day's been going, I wouldn't be surprised."

Roger passed me on his way out, and I followed him. "Hey," I said, hurrying to keep up, "Hey, I reckon I'd better go on home, don't you? I mean, I got things to do and all, and I don't want to get in the way here."

Roger ignored me as he opened the cruiser door. He picked up the radio mic and connected with the dispatcher, asked for backup to a larceny investigation and a drug arrest. When he was through, he sat for a minute more, gazing out across Crossley Creek and points west.

"Roger?" I said. "Did you need to talk to me about something?"

He looked at me for a second as if he couldn't remember who I was. "Lord, Norton, what a mess. What am I going to do with that man? He don't have a mean bone in his body, and there's not a man born who could get the better of him in a trade, but there he sits, handcuffs on because he lit up a joint right in front of a uniformed police officer."

He paused, but I couldn't speak. I wanted to leave so bad my feet were tingling.

"And he stuck a gun worth ten thousand dollars under

the couch. Can you believe that?" Roger looked up at me then, but I still couldn't answer. That gun worth ten thousand dollars was hanging in plain view of Roger and any person driving up Lonesome Gap Road, not fifteen feet from where I was standing. All he had to do was turn his head, look straight through his windshield and across the loose hay and pop cans in the bed of my truck, and there it was. I fought hard to keep from looking at it, myself.

And he thought Pres was crazy for hiding it under the couch.

It's funny what can pop into you head when you're under a lot of stress. Without any warning at all my mouth opened and I said, "Sherlock Holmes."

"What?" Roger frowned at me.

It had suddenly come to me that in the story it was Sherlock Holmes who'd found the letter hidden in plain view, among a bunch of other letters. I clenched my jaws shut. If I didn't take charge, they might say anything. Confess, even.

Roger and me both waited to hear what I'd say next, but his radio crackled and he turned back to it. I made out something about a backup being in the area, maybe arriving momentarily.

When he'd hung the mic back on its stand, Roger seemed to have come back to himself. He got out of the car and slammed the door, and hitched up his belt. He was aimed for the house, but he paused and said, "I was going to ask you when Chester and Judy were getting back from their vacation. I heard about a good trout stream over in Hanley County, I thought he and I should try out."

"Oh! Oh, Chester and Judy, they're supposed to get back on Tuesday, I think. I'll tell him, soon's as I see him. Or I could leave a note in their house. I've been feeding their dogs and stuff."

"All right. Thanks." Roger started for the porch.

"Hey! Can I go now? Roger?"

He stopped, paused, turned around and walked back to

me. "Why don't you take Norma and her little girl some-where for a while? They don't need to be here with all the uproar. It would scare that little girl, maybe."

"Yeah, sure, I'll take them somewhere. Like, for the night or what?" I was having a brief, bright image of the three of us driving right out of the state, gun and all, to start new lives together in some place warm and sunny.

"No, Norton! She'll have to be questioned. Just take them to the store for an ice cream or something, just drive them around for about an hour. Then get right back, okay?"

"Okay." He started to the house again, but I said, "Uh, Roger?" and he stopped and looked back, sort of impatiently. "Could you move your car, please?"

"Here." He pulled a set of keys on a ring out of his pocket and tossed them to me. "Move it yourself, and be careful."

"Okay." Imagine Roger trusting me with the keys to his police car. And me a thief.

I backed his car and pulled it onto the grass beside my truck. Before I had its engine turned off, Norma and Angel were coming out of the house. We all got in the truck and I started backing out. I put my arm on top of the seat so I could turn around and see behind me, and I accidentally touched Norma's shoulder. She turned and for the first time noticed the gun.

"James!" she shrieked, and Angel started howling and Norma clutched her up to her chest. I jerked the wheel and slammed on the brakes and killed the engine.

"What?" I yelled back. I had never raised my voice to her before, but I was pretty tense right then.

Norma was staring at me and the baby was screaming, so I took a deep breath and said again, "What?" only in a more reasonable tone, and Angel turned her volume down too.

"Is that IT?" Norma asked. She'd gone from yelling to whispering.

"Is what it?"

"That. *That.*" She nodded her head sideways, toward the

210

gun. "Is that *it*?"

I glanced towards the house, restarted the engine, started backing out. "Yes." Now I was whispering too.

"My God, I thought you'd hide it, not put it on public display!"

"I hid it the smart way." I wasn't about to tell her I'd already decided that was about the dumbest move I'd made in years, if not in my whole life.

She looked at me like I'd spoken in Japanese or something, but she just smoothed Angel's hair, and kissed the top of her head, and said, "All right, baby, that's enough. Everything's all right, hush now."

And right then, even with all the stuff going on and being scared I was going to spend the rest of my natural life in prison and even with the bad, guilty feelings I was starting to have way down in the heels of my feet or somewhere way low, I saw the way Norma's hands gentled themselves around her baby's head and back, and heard the tone she used to soothe the child, and love washed over me like a spring flood over a river rock. It was like something inside me broke and fell open. It was like I'd never even seen that child before, seen what a miracle she was, or understood just how beautiful Norma was underneath the hair and T-shirts. It was like I'd never felt anything deeply enough to understand - anything - before.

I stopped the truck and just looked at them for a few seconds. Angel's head was against her momma's chest, facing me. I reached over and let my fingertip follow the circle of one curl just above her eye. "Hey, Angel," I said. I don't think I'd ever said her name out loud, before. "I'm thinking maybe an ice cream is what I need right now. Think you could use some ice cream too?"

She sat there and considered. She looked at me hard and I couldn't breathe, I was so afraid she'd turn her face away. But before I turned blue from lack of oxygen she gave me about a two-second smile, and nodded.

I closed my eyes and found tears in them. I reached for Norma and pulled her and Angel close and held them hard. Then I started the truck and backed out of Pres's driveway. All the way to the store I held Norma's hand, and Angel's fat little knee rested against my hand, too.

Just below Pres's house we met another sheriff's car, and it sort of brought me back to reality. I may have just discovered Love, but there was still a stolen gun hanging in my truck, and I still didn't have money to take Norma and Angel out of Highlands County, and there was still Pres, back there with Roger, criminal and victim both, and Norma's uncle to boot.

We drove to the store without talking and walked in together. There was a big group of people standing and leaning around the checkout counter, and as soon as we came in, conversation among them stopped. I said hello to the group in general, and when I intercepted the glare Wanda had for Norma, I put my arm around Norma's shoulders. We walked through their silence to the ice cream freezer. I wasn't sure what was going on, but I hoped the events of the last hour in Pres Baugess' house hadn't had time to make it to the store yet. Surely not that quick.

But I was wrong. We took our ice creams to the back of the store, to the corner where the loafers usually sat. While we were there and I was letting my fudgesickle drip on my hand because I couldn't quit watching Angel digging little bites of ice cream (chocolate, my favorite too) out of a cardboard cup with a plastic spoon, I heard a crackle from Wanda's police scanner and then, "...residence of Woodrow Baugess, 1842 Lonesome Gap Road, Crossley community. I'll be out of my car while I assist in the investigation of a probable grand larceny..." and then the deputy gave a detailed description of the ten thousand dollar gun.

The group at the counter kept quiet while they eyed each other, then finally Enoch straightened up and strolled back

212

to where we were. "Hello, Norton," he said.

"Hey, 'Noch."

"Who's these two purty wimmin you got with ye today?"

He knew as well as I did, who they were. "This is my girl-friend and her old woman." Angel looked up at me and gave me a piece of a smile. It made my hand shake, and drops of melted fudgesickle patted onto the floor. Norma handed me a napkin.

'Noch sat on the old church pew under the window. He took a drag on his cigarette and then looked at Norma. "I hear they was some trouble up at your Uncle Pres's house today."

Norma flicked her eyes at me, but didn't speak. She wiped a line of brown drool off Angel's chin.

"What kind of trouble did you hear about?" I asked, keeping my voice steady.

"Well, of course, everybody knowed he kept some nerve medicine on hand all the time. Sort of a traditional remedy, you might say. Sort of like ginseng and moonshine. But who do you reckon woulda robbed Pres? Did you get a look at this gun?" He was asking Norma.

She just shook her head.

'Noch shook his head in agreeable sorrow. "I tell you, it's a-getting so a man can't hardly leave his door unlocked to go to the toilet. It's no telling who might stroll in and rob you blind, before you can finish your business." Silence dragged on while 'Noch smoked and considered the sorry state of personal safety in Highlands County, where there hadn't been a case of anonymous crime in twelve years. If somebody got shot at or their car borrowed without permission, it was always by a member of the family. Until now. Until Pres had his one-of-only-two-in-the-world gun stolen.

I heard the front door slam and looked up as Wanda, who had evidently just come in, hurried past the group at the counter and into the office. She turned around and came back out, and just for a split second she looked me straight in the eye, and there was something in her look that I recognized. She lifted the telephone off the counter and carried it into the office with her, and shut the door.

I dropped the remains of my ice cream into the trash can, and scooped up Angel in one arm like I'd carried her around for her whole life. I got her cup of ice cream in the other hand. "Let's go," I said to Norma, and I didn't even look to see if she was coming. I walked up the aisle, out the door, and straight to the truck. Norma got there just as I did, and she opened the door and got in. I handed the baby to her, and the cup of ice cream, and slammed the door. I quick-stepped it around the front of the truck, got in, started the engine, and was a quarter-mile up the road before Angel figured out she ought to have protested being picked up like that. She turned to Norma and opened her mouth to cry, but Norma put in a spoonful of ice cream. Angel had to either eat the ice cream or lose it as she opened her mouth to cry, so, being a sensible child and ice cream a rare treat because Norma was against her eating too much sugar, she swallowed and was contented by the sweet chocolate.

"Where are we going?" Norma asked.

"Back to Pres's house."

She didn't say another word. Soon we were back in the driveway, the engine ticking as it cooled off. I turned and looked at Norma, who looked back at me, but I couldn't think of a word to say. I got the gun off the rack and got out. I went around and opened Norma's door. She held Angel in her arms as she slid down off the seat, and she stood there between me and the pickup and just then the sun slid down into Webster's Gap and stuck a big long arm across the valley and pushed its fingers through Norma's and Angels' hair. It gave them haloes. They were so beautiful, and fragile. I leaned forward and held them against me with the arm that wasn't holding the gun, and I felt Norma leaning into me, too.

"Will you marry me, Norma? Will you and Angel be my

214

family, and let me take care of you?"

Norma pulled back a little, and looked up at me. I was easy and calm now. I knew what I wanted. I knew what was important, and if Norma said no now, I would ask again later. I would keep asking and doing the important stuff, until she said yes. But I wanted her to say yes right then, yes to me the way I was without waiting to see how I might turn out.

"Yes," she said.

The sun went on down below the ridge and pulled out of my two girls' hair, but I felt warm and light, myself. I sucked in a big chestful of air. I know I was smiling like a possum in pokeberries, I could feel my cheek muscles stretch. "All right then," I said, and I pressed my forehead against Norma's. Angel raised her hand and rubbed the back of the plastic spoon over my cheek. It was cool and slimy, so I knew I had either ice cream or spit, or maybe both, across my face. I turned my head and put my lips against that little girl's wrist, and that was the sweetest, tenderest thing I had ever touched in my life. I pressed my mouth against her skin and blew out, and it made a big fart sound.

It surprised all of us, and we had a sort of delayed reaction. Then we started laughing. Angel didn't know how to take it at first, but Norma and I were carrying on so, she started laughing too. We laughed until we had to lean against the truck, to keep from falling. We laughed until tears ran down our cheeks.

Finally I caught my breath. I wiped my face in the bend of my arm, and hoisted the gun. "I've got to go take care of this," I said.

"Okay." There were still tears running down her cheeks. From laughing, I guess.

Ten years can make a lot of difference in a person's life. It was a mess, when I went into Pres's house and handed over the rifle and tried to explain it all, but finally, things got sorted out. There were no charges against me and Norma –

215

Pres didn't even seem upset about me confessing that I had taken the gun. Pres got off with about a hundred years' probation, which never seemed to make an iota of difference in the way he lived his life, except that between me and Norma and Roger and even my brother Chester, somebody made sure the paperwork was done on all his "trades," and he did stop selling pot to other people.

Angel is almost a teenager now, and she has two little brothers to contend with. We've added onto Pres's house twice, and remodeled so he has one big room for all his trade stuff, even though he doesn't do so much work anymore. And he doesn't keep guns in the house at all, because he's afraid the kids might get hold of one and hurt themselves. Or somebody else.

When we first got married, Norma and Angel and I moved to Abingdon. There was a couple of hard years there, while I went to the community college and worked on a second shift, and Norma waited tables at Shoney's. She hated putting Angel in daycare, but it worked out better than she thought it would.

By the time Angel was old enough to start school, Norma was ready to come home. I asked her how she felt about bringing up our little girl in Highlands County, where everybody knew our history from six generations back, but Norma said Angel wasn't a Baugess any more. She was a Blevins now, and that was nothing to be ashamed of.

Besides, by then Pres was needing us. The doctors had found a problem with his heart, probably there from birth, and he needed to take his pills on a regular schedule, but he forgot. So we moved in and eventually I got on with the state, and Daddy and I worked together for three years, until he retired.

I guess the oddest thing that's happened to us in these ten years has been that box of silver dollars. We got married in the church where my family has always gone, those of us who do, and Norma wore the dress all my sisters had worn and

216

handed down. It was a pretty thing, all satin and pearls and big rustly petticoats, and I have to say that Norma filled it out a little different from any of the Blevins girls.

Right before the ceremony, Pres (who gave the bride away and who had put on not only a rented suit but also clean underwear, under the careful inspection of Roger Steele, my best man) came and got me, and took me to the little Sunday school classroom where Norma was waiting.

"Children, I want to be giving you a little wedding present, here." Pres had on his old hat, and had his right arm folded across his middle, even though someone had taken away his jacket.

"Pres, you don't need to give us anything." Norma answered, because as I recall, I was struck dumb by the sight of Norma's beautiful hair made soft by that long veil and her figure rounding out that dress.

"Well, there's something I have been saving for you for a long time." I thought that was just a little bit of Pres's craziness. Norma and I had only met a few months earlier. How could he have saved something for us for a long time?

But we didn't try to correct him, and he handed Norma a brown cardboard box with a Christmas bow taped to the top. I stood close beside her as she pulled off the bow and opened the flaps. And there was that tin cracker box. And when Norma opened that, with her hands shaking so bad I thought maybe I'd have to do it, there were all those silver dollars. Just like on the day we stole Pres's gun.

Norma wouldn't look at me, or at Pres, and nobody spoke for a long stretch of time, until finally Norma's voice came out, all small and shaky.

"When I was a little bitty kid," she said, almost whispering, "and living up on the mountain in Grandpa Sam's cabin, there were cousins and kinfolks and hound dogs enough to fill three or four houses that size. And Grandpa was a fierce old man, and quick to use his cane to clear out a space around his chair, and I was scared of him. And I was scared of the dogs, and scared of most of my cousins, and Mommy wasn't hardly ever home. I was about the most scared and miserable little scrap in the world.

"One day I was trying to get away from the uproar, and I crawled under the porch of the cabin, and then I crawled on back under the house. It was cool under there, and dusky dark, and the dirt was soft as flour."

"And you found the sack," Pres said, as if we were discussing the weather and he thought it might rain.

"I found this little leather sack," Norma said, and she looked up at me. "And it had three coins in it, big heavy coins. I knew that if anybody else saw those coins, they'd take them away from me. I hadn't had anything of my very own in my whole life, and I wanted to keep them so bad, not because they were money, but just because they were mine."

Norma put her hand over her eyes and sat, all scrunched down. I looked at Pres, but he was just watching her, mouth in its usual little half-smile.

After a few minutes, Norma wiped her face and went on. "I had crawled back to the edge of the porch, to have light enough to see what I'd found. And Pres came and set down on the grass near to where I was."

"And you showed 'em to me," Pres said.

"I didn't have a friend in the world." Norma was really whispering, now. "Not one soul I loved. But I crawled out there and showed them to Pres."

Pres nodded. "And I told her, Missy, if you keep the first money you ever find, you'll always have enough."

"And I gave them to you to keep for me."

"And I kept 'em."

"It was our secret. And no matter how miserable I was, stuck off up there on the mountain without anybody paying much attention to me at all, I could think about my special coins. When Pres came around, he'd always wink at me, and nod, and I'd know they were safe. And there was somebody I shared something with."

218

"And here they are." Press leaned over and looked in the box. "Them three are on the bottom. I added to 'em, over the years. Ever once in a while I'd come across a silver dollar for a bargain, and I'd think, well, there's another one for little Missy. And I'd put 'em in the box."

He straightened up and turned around, headed for the door. "Happy wedding day," he said. "Remember now, you keep them three you found first. I reckon it's time for us to have the wedding."

I reached down and took Norma's hand for a minute, then followed Pres out the door.

It's been a funny thing about those coins. Whenever we've got to a real hard place, we've dipped into the box and sold a few. They were our first month's rent in Abingdon, and the deposit on the electricity. When I was in school and Angel got such a bad infection in her throat that we thought she might die, we sold off some coins and paid the hospital bill. We used some for part of my tuition. We've sold one or two just to buy groceries, when we were down to the last bean. But we never let go of those first three, and the others have kept coming back to us, somehow. Pres, mostly, would show up with one or two that he'd "got for a bargain." A few times, in the later years, I've come across silver dollars for sale at flea markets, and bought them, and put them in the box. They were probably not the same, exact coins we'd sold off, but they were there.

Not long ago Norma came home from the Wal-Mart with two decorative tin boxes. She went into Pres's room, where he stays mostly in bed, now, and called all the kids in. The boys hung around Norma's shoulders, and Angel got up on Pres's bed.

"Honey, don't bother your Uncle Pres," I said.

"She ain't no bother," Pres said. Same old voice, calm and steady.

I watched while Norma got out our box, and dumped all the silver dollars onto the edge of Pres's bed. She divided them into three equal piles. Then she pulled out a little old leather sack, about four inches across and six or seven inches long, soft and supple as chamois. Three big heavy coins slid out into her hand, all tarnished and gray.

"I want you all to listen to a story," she said. "It's a story about a little girl and the three coins she found, and the good magician who blessed them and put a spell on them, and who helped the little girl live happily ever after."

The kids all settled in, and Pres turned toward her too, because Norma is a rare good storyteller.

I just hope she leaves out the part about their daddy stealing the gun. Children don't need to know just everything. Not all at once.

Deb's first book

Deborah Tilson Clark, daughter of two, sister of three, wife of one, mother of two, lives in the place where her heart has ever longed to be. Her urge to write, awakened at an early age and refusing to ever, ever die a quiet death, is strong. She's learned a lot from a lot of people and in a lot of "schools," starting in her own backyard and continuing across a couple of states and a healthy variety of jobs and even during a few trips across the big waters, where a poor little Appalachian girl was never supposed to go.

This is her second published collection of short stories; the first book did well enough to make the second one happen. There are plenty more stories in her files and in her mind and heart. She's promised her daughter that the next one will have more magic and more darkness, to make the light show up better. The one after that will have a possum, or an armadillo, or a cat who is the Guardian against Death. We'll see.

"Authentic voice - I don't read much fiction, but I like to read "local" authors to see how accurately they capture life in these mountains. This author definitely gets it, and transmits it in colorful, flavorful descriptions. I could relate to every character as similar to someone I know or have known. I read one story at a time, and I was sad to realize there were no more. I hope there will be more stories coming soon from this talented writer."   Kathy Cole

"Superb, masterful storytelling. More, please! Superb storytelling exploring many facets of the human condition, with a marvelous touch of O. Henry. The voices bounced around in my ears, thanks to the author's loving, unobtrusive mastery of the timbre, cadence and vocabulary of mountain folk speech. I chuckled and admired my way from story to story. More please!"   Rester

"For an insightful and inside view of the Southern Appalachians, this is it! No more of Vance's reporting on his dysfunctional family in Hillbilly Elegy, this is an insightful and inside view of the true Appalachia. Short stories that leaves one in wonder of the realities of the mountains in SW Virginia. Great read!"   Jerry A. Moles

"If a book could be a blanket, this would be it. I very much enjoyed the narrative style Deborah writes with! Feels like sitting down with an old friend and listening to them tell a story they love to tell. :) Interesting characters that draw you in with their quirks, flaws, and innate humanity! A good read, especially accompanied by a hot cup of tea and a warm cat." Hols

"Excellent stories - I loved all the stories, and my co-worker I loaned it to has gushed about the ones he's read too. Well-written, literate, warm, touching, deep, with just a touch of strange to keep things interesting."   Jess

www.ingramcontent.com/pod-product-compliance
Lightning Source LLC
Chambersburg PA
CBHW071331250626
47159CB00004B/1566